THE WAY IT WAS

Nostalgic Tales of Hotrods and Romance

by Chuck Klein

with

Illustrations by: *Bill Lutz*

Introduction by: *Al Drake*

BeachHouse Books

Chesterfield Missouri, USA

Copyright

Graphics Credits:

Graphics Credits:
Cover design by Dr. Bud Banis. based around drawings by Bill Lutz with text and enhancements by Dr. Bud Banis.

Publication date August, 2003
ISBN 1-888725-86-9 Regular print BeachHouse Books Edition

First Printing, August, 2003

Library of Congress Cataloging-in-Publication Data
Klein, Chuck.
  The way it was : nostalgic tales of hotrods and romance / by Chuck Klein; with illustrations by Bill Lutz ; introduction by Al Drake.
    p. cm.
ISBN 1-888725-86-9 (Beachhouse Books regular print : alk. paper) --
ISBN 1-888725-87-7 (MacroPrintBooks 16 point : alk. paper)
  1. Love stories, American. 2. Historical fiction, American. 3. Young adults--Fiction. 4. Hot rods--Fiction. I. Lutz, Bill. II. Title.

  PS3561.L3425W395 2003
  813'.54--dc22

                 2003017771

BeachHouse
Books

www.beachhousebooks.com

an Imprint of

Science & Humanities Press

PO Box 7151

Chesterfield, MO 63006

(636) 394-4950

www.beachhousebooks.com

For my grandsons, Chas and Adam, and The Knights of the Twentieth Century

PREFACE

Henry Gregor Felsen was among the first to write, circa 1952, about the then new phenomena, hot rodding. His books, *HOT ROD, STREET ROD*, et. al., not only inspired young car aficionados, but more importantly they opened the door of reading to the youth of the era. As a teen-ager, I thought reading was for squares - until I discovered Felsen's male-oriented, car-intensive novels.

Recently, I wrote Hank asking if he would write the introduction to this book. Over a period of about a year we corresponded, bonding on our mutual interest in reading and cars. He agreed to pen an introduction. When I hadn't heard from him after a few months, I wrote again. I was not prepared for the response - a missive from his widow! Hank, in his 80th year, had passed away a few weeks before. One of the greatest compliments I have ever received came from the editor of Street Rod Action who has run a number of the stories in their magazine. The editor told me: "If Hank Felsen was still writing, this (my stories) is what he would be writing."

Some of my Walter Mitty/Felsen style scenarios are based on actual happenings and events. The other only-in-America yarns most likely did happen...or should have. The story, LAST KNIGHT, is factual inasmuch as there was a Knights hot rod club, they did hold a reunion in the mid 1980's and they do have a tontine. CLOSE ENCOUNTERS, SUMMER 1957 and TEXAS/NEW MEXICO, 1961 are true accounts of personal experiences. My description of

American the Beautiful in the story, AMERICA, has been honored with publication in the United States Congressional Record (Vol. 138, No. 104, Page 2220). All of these historically and technically correct stories are void of graphic sex and explicit language.

The illustrations are by the most talented, Bill Lutz. Bill's unique ability to transform my stories into pictures and his deep knowledge of hot rods made for a satisfying and complete package.

My hope is the youth of the next generation - the ones who think reading is uncool - will find this work in their school library and discover "inner cool" thus perpetuating the legacy of Hank Felsen.

Chuck Klein, 2003

INTRODUCTION

Since Chuck Klein has invoked Henry Gregor Felsen in his preface, I have to say that Felsen's work was a touchstone of my youthful reading. I read his novels during the 1950s and later wrote a novel, **BEYOND THE PAVEMENT**; it owed much to Felsen's work as I realized when I re-read his novels during the 1980s. I interviewed Felsen in 1984 and again in 1988, and somewhere along the line we became friends. Felsen was not really a car guy, and the magic of his fiction is that he was able to capture the sense of what it was like to be a young man obsessed with modified cars, usually in a small town in the Midwest. There was the loneliness, the <u>angst</u>, the desire for motion, the need to move away from everything that was holding one back: speed verses stasis.

Felsen wrote his books in the 'Fifties, and the events he wrote about were contemporary with the emerging sport of hot rodding. But what is this desire to recapture the sense of the 'Fifties some forty plus years later? Well, I think it was a wonderful decade, and cars were part of what made it wonderful. When I think of the 'Fifties I think of a lazy afternoon in the hammock in the backyard, drinking a glass of cherry Kool-Aid and reading back issues of **Hot Rod Magazine**. Through the space beside the garage I could look at my '29 A- V8 roadster and day-dream of the impossible: getting a pair of aluminum Offy heads, driving it to California, making a run at El Mirage. I swear that days were much longer during the 'Fifties, and there was time for working on a car as well as day-dreaming, plus some cruising in the evening. There was also that new music, Rock 'n Roll, although I'm not sure exactly when we began calling it that. There were numerous drive-in restaurants, places where you could go to show off your car while you ate a package of fries and drank a Coke. While it's true that some people may have been oppressed, America was a great country during the 'Fifties. Jobs were plentiful, everyone seemed to have some money, and the factories were turning out great products, such as the 1955 Chevrolet, the Corvette, the Thunderbird. Life seemed to be the idyllic version seen in advertisements and on television. Families seemed to stay together, women seemed to be happy, and certainly there were no weird diseases to worry about. Whenever the world around me becomes too awful I retreat to the Fabulous 'Fifties and live in my head. Some pop psychologist will accuse me of allowing the inner child to regress to a safe spot and I'll have to agree — who needs reality?

I can't speak for Chuck Klein's reasons for placing his stories in the 'Fifties, but some of the above might apply. I met Chuck Klein on the page when I read his novel, *CIRCA 1957*, a few years ago. This novel, which I recommend, is the story of Paul Auer and his close friends during the latter part of the 'Fifties. Although still in school, they're car nuts and their lives revolve around cars — and, of course, girls. Paul is fifteen, and longs for a car, so his father buys him a Crosley sedan!. His other friends and some older guys either have or later get cars — generally of the kind we all know and love, modified cars, rods and customs — and Paul moves on up to a Corvette. But the book is also concerned with relationships, school, the dating scene and other things that we associate with that dance from adolescence to young adulthood. One thing that I noticed about the book, and I feel that Chuck Klein is a real stickler on these things, the songs and sayings were true to the time period. It's fiction, but it has the authority of fact.

Several stories in this collection pick up on the material in **CIRCA 1957**. The same characters show up in the "Announcer", and "Summer of '57" is, as I recall, and excerpt from the novel. In "The Alumni" two middle-aged men meet on the job and begin to reminisce about Cincinnati, the town they grew up in during the late 'Fifties; as a result we get information about characters in **CIRCA 1957** as well as characters in stories in this collection, such as Jack and Natalie from "The Vette". This kind of cross-referencing is fun and it adds dimension to the stories.

Other stories strongly evoke the sense of the late 'Fifties. In "My Girl" both Terry and Pete like Brittney; while she seems interested in Terry, and promises to see him, at the end she comes to Pete and climbs willingly into the front seat of his '51 Chev convertible mild custom. This is a subtle display of the myth of feminine evil. In "Train Run" young Tommy does himself in without help from anyone else when he races a steam locomotive to the crossing. "America", more of a sketch than a story, is an unabashed celebration of the greatness of this country by a character named Bucky who, in 1957, is recalled to active duty and drives from Kansas to San Diego. "The Hero" is set in the present but when Carl Sampson is stopped by a cop he recalls the story's central event, set in 1957.

Several of these stories I first read when they were published in **Street Rod Action**. The car magazines publish almost no fiction—I had a story in **Rod Action** in 1972, and there were none in the magazine for the next twenty years!— and so I was curious what the reaction would be. Editors and publishers have told me that they avoid fiction in car magazines because rodders don't like to read. I know this isn't true, because I'm a hot rodder and I love to read. As a result of getting stories into print, Chuck Klein got some very positive mail, which the editors published in the letters page. One thing I think the readers enjoyed were the twist endings to several of the stories. I won't delineate the plot or untwist the endings because that might spoil the effect for the reader, but check out stories like "Day Dreams", "The Hero" and "The Vette".

Other stories appeal to readers for other reasons. "The Pickup" is narrated in the first person by a 1937 Ford pickup; this anthropomorphic voice tells the life story of the truck, from its birth to the despair of the junkyard to its rebirth as a street rod. "Last Knight", while its ritual will intrigue you, its ending will surprise you.

The variety of the stories insures something for everyone. The same can be said for the drawings by Bill Lutz that accompany and complement the stories, and which add a wonderful visual dimension to the narratives.

Albert Drake

Portland, Oregon

LIST OF STORIES

THE PICK-UP

From some quarry deep in Wisconsin, via cavernous ships, came the iron ore. Compounded, mixed and incorporated with other raw ingredients from mines as far away as the continent of Africa; the River Rouge's open hearth furnaces formed the very heart of America's rolling stock. But it took the conscientious and loving care of the meticulous assembly line workers to collate these unique organs and create the real soul of each vehicle.

Early in January, 1937, number 3846, a pick-up truck, received its "soul". She came down the line and under the tender guardianship of the day shift, was bestowed the larger 85 horsepower V8 engine, Vermilion Red paint with black stripe and black "solid" wheels.

I felt good and rode proud and tall on the train to St. Louis where an elderly gentleman gently drove me to the show room at the Ford dealership just west of downtown. I didn't have to wait long, like the plainer coupes and sedans, some of which had to remain out in the rain and cold. On January 22, Number 3846, that's me, became the property of Mr. Silas T. Wentworth, a lanky and muscular farmer from up-state Missouri.

Silas T., his wife, Priscilla, and their son, Jamie, took pride in their first "new" car. The depression had been difficult but through hard work and very austere living they prospered. I heard Silas T. talking about how I, as their new addition to the family, would enable him to increase his market deliveries three fold over the horse and wagon.

Even hauling hogs to market was no strain for my powerful flathead engine, and return trips, empty except for a few supplies, made life easy and enjoyable. Silas T. changed my oil and greased me on a very regular basis and Jamie kept me clean. The missus even made seat covers for me.

Things changed in 1940. Jamie turned 16 and began driving me to school and other places. Silas T. bought a heavy duty, dual-rear-wheel truck who soon became the pride of the family. Jamie was hard on me with all his quick starts and fast driving, but I knew I was having a better life than some of the others I'd see stuck by the roadway or — in junk yards! Once, when we went to town, I saw a sedan that had been right behind me on the assembly line. That sedan was now a police car with a spot light and a two-tone paint job. And, even though she was just a sedan, she turned up her nose at common pick-ups.

Jamie had a special girl and they often went out for rides together, only they spent more time parking than actually riding. They talked of marriage and how he was sure his dad would give him the pick-up and sign on a note so as he could buy the old Potter place.

We had a lot of fun, the three of us. Jamie and I once raced a Chevrolet out on the East River Road. We sprayed gravel all over that snooty looking Chevy and beat him by a country mile by doing almost 90! Mabel, that's his girl, made him promise never to do that again because they would need me for farm use.

It was in my bed, on blanket covered straw, during the summer of 1942, they got engaged. Mabel was scared but Jamie promised to love her forever. They talked about the kids they wanted and how they would fix up the old Potter place, even a stall in the barn for me, when he got back.

It all seemed so perfect except that I was getting tired and one of my springs was starting to sag a little. Jamie sure looked sharp in that uniform with all those shiny buttons. I don't know why everyone was crying, even Mabel. The two men drove me to town. They shook hands, hugged, and Jamie patted me on my fender before he got into a bus. Silas T. brought me back, parked me in the lean-to where the surrey used to be, and disconnected my battery.

It was a very long time before anyone opened that barn door again. Silas T. Wentworth, on that cold and windy day, looked gaunt and sad. A plump pimply faced kid, Mr. Wentworth called him Butch, kicked my tires, shook my fenders and looked me over then handed my first master a check. The next day Butch returned, winched me onto a trailer, and took me back into the big city.

Much to my surprise Butch began cleaning me and showing me off to his friends who came to visit the garage. It seems the garage is the headquarters for the Piston Busters Car Club. It wasn't long before Butch and friends had yanked my old and tired engine and with a little drilling, grinding and welding — the welding hurt — installed an almost new Corvette engine! Wow! Butch sanded off the old faded paint and applied a bright yellow primer, converted to hydraulic brakes and added fancy chrome wheels with new white-wall tires. Boy, if only my old assembly line mates could see me now! I'll bet even the police car would be envious.

Every time we went to the Big Boy drive-in all the other guys would gather around and admire me. Sundays, we'd go to the drag strip, and though it hurt to have that much pressure put on my rails, I loved it. Sometimes we even brought home a trophy! The speeds we reached were far more than Jamie and I had ever dreamed. Things weren't all that great though. Some of my body mounts were wearing out and the high output V8 engine, twisting against my rusty frame, gave me a lot of pain. I was sure that someday I wouldn't be able to keep it together.

Other than that, life was pretty good — at least I didn't have to haul any smelly ol' hogs or dusty hay. But I did carry a few kegs of beer and a bunch of club members more than once. Butch always kept me in a garage and never let anyone else drive me, 'cept Suzie, his girl, and that was only on one occasion.

Late in the spring of '60 we were coming out of a high speed turn on the new subdivision road when one of my shock mounts broke. It caused me to lose control and we slammed into a stone wall bending my front axle and crumpling one fender. Butch broke my windshield with his head and leaked a sticky red oil all over my cowl and hood. He lay there for a long time before one of those stuck-up police cars and a shiny new ambulance arrived. Then things happened pretty fast and next thing I know they tow me to, of all places, a junk yard!

With a half century's worth of the formerly new and proud modes of transportation to trade stories with, I was never lonely. And though I was not happy with my situation at least I had had a more complete and exciting life than most of the other "junkers". But, I still had a lot of life left in me and I didn't want to spend forever with these rusty heaps.

Oh, sometimes somebody would come and look me over — shake me or kick my now flat tires, but mostly they just wanted my parts. As the years rolled by I lost my steering wheel, the good front fender, my radiator, engine — it was only a Chevy — and other items. My interior rotted away and the faded yellow primer — Butch never did get around to that metal flake paint job he had promised — rusted through in many places. At least I had the other cars to keep me company not like being shut in the Wentworth barn all alone. A once majestic LaSalle, the leader of the yard, because of the shade from a Maple tree that grew out of his trunk, became my best friend. He loved to tell of the times he chauffeured the Mayor and his important guests and friends around.

Sometimes you get lucky. I had never resigned myself to the junk yard mentality of my fellow prisoners as I always believed I'd be rescued. It was hot, late in the fall of 1989, when I winked a goodbye to the huge LaSalle. Craig, a jovial man who looked to be almost as old as Silas T. had looked the last time I saw him, carefully loaded me onto a trailer.

My next home was, well, better than the factory. It was clean, brightly lighted and had some very sophisticated tools and machinery. I just knew Craig and I were going be the best of friends. It took over two years, but in that time I was reborn! Even my assembly line mates would hardly recognize me. Craigie — that's what his wife calls him — took me all apart, I mean every nut, bolt, flange, bushing — everything. He stripped my metal bare and then what he didn't primer and paint he chromed. I also received new fiberglass fenders, a new dropped front axle, a chopped top — it only hurt a little — rolled & pleated naugahyde interior and — ugh — another Chevy engine, but complete with supercharger. I loved it. I wanted to go by the junk yard and show-off.

In no time at all Craigie sold me to a man who I'm ashamed to identify. A man whose smile never reaches his eyes. Almost every weekend he loads me into a closed trailer and tows me to a car show. He ropes me off so none of the countless admirers can caress my 27 hand- rubbed coats of lacquer or fondle my cute little stainless and wood steering wheel. Ah, this should be the life, no more hauling of any kind, frame stressing races or even getting rained on. Only trouble is I hate it. My engine, even thought it's not a Ford, has never been started. Once when he had me sitting in his driveway a few of his friends came by in "real" hot-rods with engines that worked — I was so embarrassed. I long for just sitting at a Big Boy and maybe a few wheel spins in the lot, the wind at 100 per or the pleasure of a master who knows how to handle a street rod.

Say...if you see me at one of those frilly, pseudo-hot-rod, indoor car shows, make my owner an offer he can't refuse, put some guts in my mill and lets do it! I won't let you down.

LAST KNIGHT

In the beginning was Elvis and Smokey
the Everly's Richie and Fats
four-on-the-floor or three-on-the-tree
and DARLING COME SOFTLY TO ME....

The young man, in his late teens, pulled into the driveway, eager to show his father and great grandfather his latest acquisition, a '32 Ford. Almost at the same time a delivery man arrived with a package. Taking the carefully wrapped box, with the word "FRAGILE" stamped in red on all sides, into the library of the ancient Tudor style house, he approached a much older man seated in a leather wingback.

"Pop." Then a little louder, "Grandpa, come outside for a minute I want to show you my new car. It's got all the extras."

The old timer knew cars. He had studied, and in some cases rubbed shoulders with, the best of the early engineers, customizers and racers. Men with the immortalized names of Iskenderian, Duntov, Barris, Fangio, Vukovich....

After the ritualistic inspection of the male bonding medium the two men returned to the den where the younger remembered the package. "I almost forgot, Pop, this came for you a little while ago."

"What is it Sonny?" the old man asked, settling into his overstuffed chair.

"I don't know Pop. It's from some law office back east and it sounds like it has liquid in it. You getting your Geritol by mail now?" The great grandson joked.

Staring at the proffered package the old man pushed back further into the cushions of the chair as if trying to distance himself from it. His mouth dropped open... "oh my God", escaped in an barely audible, raspy whisper.

"Grandpa, what's wrong? Are you okay?" The young gentleman crossed the room to take this ancient man's hand and search his frightened stare. "What is it, Pop?"

As recollections of events, forever melded to the sentimental portions of his mind, were forced to the present, the great grandfather's eyes soon began refocusing to a new intensity. "Get a couple of glasses and some ice, Sonny - and call your Dad in here. I've got a story to tell you."

A man with graying hair and his teenage son watched the great grandfather, in his 96th year, carefully and ceremoniously unwrap the package. Inside, sealed and encased in a solid wood box with a glass front panel, was a bottle of whisky. Attached to the outside of this shrine was a small brass hammer and a pouch. From this pouch he pulled a sheet of paper containing a list of names - names that had lines drawn through each, save one.

It was a very long time ago that they had met for the last time - a sort of reunion and farewell to one of the members who had but a short time to live.

Pretensions and pressures were checked at the door that night. Whatever problems they faced outside seemed far away and not important. Maybe it was seeing a "best" friend for the first time in two or three decades or just that deep feeling that only comes from the knowledge that to this group each truly belonged. They all knew that this assembly was just this night only and never again would they all be together. Maybe it came with the understanding that these were their roots and the distinct sensation of having come home again. Perhaps it was the familiarity and companionship of old friends, whose dues were also paid in full. It was a most memorable occasion.

It wasn't a large gathering, but 21 men out of a possible 36 wasn't too bad for an informal reunion. Some had died, some couldn't be found, most were graying and pot bellied, but all had, at one time, belonged to the KNIGHTS OF THE TWENTIETH CENTURY. Born so many years ago in a back alley garage of a Midwestern American city, The KNIGHTS hot rod club was not unlike other clubs of guys of that era. Back when rock & roll was in its infancy and fast cars had to be built by hand, the members bonded together to learn, help each other and talk engines, cars and speed. It was exciting being the center of attention during this era of historic automotive and musical upheaval.

...Big Bopper and Ben E. King
and LOVE IS A MANY SPLENDORED THING

"Here, you do it Sonny," the old man said handing the brass hammer to his great grandson.

Uncapping the bottle, which had been freed by breaking the glass front and without lifting his eyes from the list, the old man in his articulate way, began to pour forth a tale as if he had been rehearsing it all his life.

"Moonie, that's what they called me because I was the first to have Moon wheel covers on my rod, a '34 roadster that I had stuffed a Caddy engine into. It had a dropped front axle, chopped windshield and sported three-deuces on the engine. Though I never got it completely finished it ran one-oh-three point six in the quarter mile. Not that this was the fastest in the club, but still very respectable. I didn't drive the roadster on the street much because something was always breaking so I kept a stock '39 Ford as my everyday car. The '39 was battered and shabby and second gear was stripped but, it ran quite reliably - those old flatheads would just run forever. The only thing I hated about that old relic was the hot, scratchy mohair seats. I got my share of carpet burns on my elbow trying to put my arm around a girl.

"Ah...the girls. It seems that we built and raced the cars to impress the girls and then whenever one of the guys had made enough of an impression she'd up and marry him and that would be the end of his hot rodding. Brides and all the 'comes-with' things associated with marriage probably contributed more to the demise of hot rodders and their clubs than anything else.

"You boys should have seen my bride! She was just about the prettiest thing that ever rode shotgun in an open roadster. I met her at a club dance - a sock hop we called it. She wore dungarees with the cuffs rolled up, in giant folds, almost to her knees. Her oversized shirt must have been her daddy's white dress button-down which also had huge folds of the sleeves all the way up her arm. The shirt tails were tied in a knot at her tiny waist, the slightest view of smooth soft skin barely visible. She wore her hair in a flip and she just had that fresh scrubbed look about her. Quite the opposite of me with my axle greased ducktails and form-fitted pink shirt with string tie and pleated slacks of charcoal gray. We rocked and rolled to the likes of Fat's Domino, Dale Wright, Buddy Holly and Larry Williams and when she put her head under my chin to 'Sixteen Candles' I knew it was something special. It was. Last week it would have been our 72nd anniversary...if she were still alive."

"Grandpa," the impatient teenager interrupted, "What about the bottle?"

"I'm comin' to that, Sonny. Don't rush me. Like I was sayin', it was at this gathering when we all got together for that one last time to say goodbye to Freddie. Now, nothing lasts forever, and by age 50 Freddie had developed a terminal case of cancer. Knowing that he was a short timer he kept himself busy hunting us down and planning this assembly to unite us for one last time and to establish his gift as a tontine - the bottle from which we are drinking at this very moment. He said he won the fifth at a club dance and being a teetotaler, just put it away. Freddie was Jewish and for that solemn affair he gave us a little insight into these ancient teachings. It was such a somber and commemorative occasion that I still remember his final words to us. Here was this dying compatriot, frail and weak, who looked each one of us in the eye as he decreed: 'In our faith it is believed that on Rosh Hashanah, the New Year, it is written; on Yom Kippur, The Day of Atonement, it is sealed:

How many shall pass on,
How many shall come to be,
Who shall live to see ripe age,
And who shall not,
Who shall live,
And who shall die;

and so it must be, that only the last surviving member of THE KNIGHTS, the KNIGHTS OF THE TWENTIETH CENTURY, may toast his fellow members with - and savor the nectar of this - this last man bottle.'"

With a sigh of finality his still steady hand, rough, dried and cracked like a cheap paint job that had crystallized, picked up the small doubles glass. Using both hands, and not unlike how one would make an offering, raised the glass to just slightly above his head whispering, "I'll see you soon fellahs, keep 'em tuned up."

Warmed by the energy of the aged whiskey the old man rose from the security of his wingback and shuffled to the leaded windows overlooking the springtime embraced driveway. Just for an instant he was sure he saw Freddie waving from his NINETEEN thirty-two Ford, the one with the hopped-up Chevy engine and the plaque that said KNIGHTS, dangling from the back bumper. But, a deliberate wipe of the hand across his tear filling eyes revealed it was only his great grandson's...brand new TWENTY thirty-two Ford.

GO-CARTERS

The cross-state hot rod club dance he attended
with never a thought of finding one to marry.
A pretty smile and a warmth he did meet
when eyes locked with a lady named Carrie.

Costumed for Halloween were they
as they danced to recorded soundtrack.
He decked out in twenties motif,
she as a sorceress in stunning black.

In conversations oblivious to others
twice his hand she did touch.
That caused a quickened heart
which he liked very much.

Comparing notes of commonalities,
he listened for hours to this pretty miss.
Though sometimes his mind wandered
and wondered what it'd be like to kiss.

Back home so far away
now he had a reason to make,
a hot rod flat-head Merc that
when finished to her it would take.

Meticulously he fitted a
full race Clay Smith Cam,
in addition to other goodies
he would carefully cram.

Of his interest he wrote
'cuz long distance cost too much,
and he needed every penny for
carbs, valves, tie rods and such.

In prose as beautiful as her face
she wrote of rock & roll devotion,
and hot rod cars and a certain
fellow who awakened deep emotion.

The nights were tiring ecstasy
as he tossed and turned sans sleep,
'cuz he couldn't stop thinking of
the lady whose company he'd like to keep.

When sleep finally did come
he dreamed in his heart of hearts,
of the day when they would make
a few little riders for go-carts

Though only in primer and
not finished at all,
he planned to drive 'cross state
to see this lovely doll.

Frivolously he spent the LD money
so as he could learn,
if it was he she also
did pine for and yearn.

He enjoyed talking with her
she seemed like the kind of girl,
he would like to know
and hopefully make her toes curl.

They agreed to meet the
very next weekend.
If only he could find
someone with money to lend.

She wrote back of how
she wanted again to meet,
on the coming Saturday eve
because she thought him very neat.

They both looked forward to then
with euphoric anticipation,
to meet and greet
for mutual participation.

He opened the rod up on the back stretch
near the old Cutter place.
The hopped up V8 gave him a thrill
almost as good as Carrie's face.

Reaching over seventy in second
he slammed hard into top gear.
The coupe was solid and at well over
a hundred there was only joy and no fear.

The primered Merc with ported and
polished block, three-deuces and dual pipes,
would soon look as good as it ran
when finished in flames and pinstripes.

Weeks of letters and a phone call
displayed a beauty of the inner kind.
The tête-à-tête revealed an attractiveness
both were happy to again find.

The evening was magic as they
talked and held hands,
like life time lovers while
listening to juke-box bands.

Not of the same faith was she
though sweet sixteen, honest and wise,
and to the rod builder
quite an outstanding prize.

After Cokes at a Big Boy
all too briefly they squeezed,
which definitely felt good
he sure hoped her it also pleased.

Forsaking the custom paint job
he took after school work,
to help pay the toll calls
that now became a nightly perk.

Life is seldom without trauma
even teenagers have pain.
It was the call from her father
that almost made him insane.

Faith was what her daddy
did object to so strong,
and they could not continue.
To him it was all very wrong.

Into rod building he delved
flush with after school money,
to make the best of the best
though he missed his honey.

The forty-nine with souped engine
was now near ready and done,
for the drag strip races
but without her it would not be fun.

The anguish and hurt
from his heart did pour,
writing unanswered letters
of how he did want more.

It was not just the touching
though it was like... wow
but they were so compatible,
even spiritually, then and now

The door is closing fast
too bad it did not last.
Fired by a very romantic spell,
how sad their love failed to gel.
Painful lows at end of magic eight weeks,
overshadowed by ultra high peaks.
Follow your heart,
or forever part.

****

At the strip that glorious day
his D-Gas coupe turned in eighty-nine, nine.
But elation was nothing compared
to seeing her in the spectator line.

From home she had run
after finding his missives,
hidden by well meaning parents
to keep her submissive.

They talked, they hugged, they loved.
She wanted to right away mate.
He thought both too young
but promised to wait 'till 1958.

He brought her home in
the hub-cap-less and numbered rod.
Her daddy was impressed with
his honor and gave them a nod.

The Merc they did ride until go-carters
arrived producing higher highs.
Then it was into a stock sedan, but they
really just rode pinnacles of contented sighs.

Today the go-carters
have go-carters of their own,
and Carrie and the hot rodder
now revel in the seeds they have sown.

THE SPIRIT OF THANKSGIVING

"John, now listen to me and be sure you get a nice big fat one. Do you hear me?" the shrill woman's voice chased him all the way to the truck.

He didn't need to answer. After 17 years he could tell the rhetorical advice and questions from the important ones. He just hoped the little pick-up would make it out back of Mason City to the turkey farm. Ever since his son had become interested in hot rodding the old truck had not been the same. Of all things, the V8 now had two carburetors on it! The gas consumption had to be twice as high and it didn't seem to start as easily as it used to. He wished Jeff had spent his money and time fixing things that really needed fixing — like the radiator. It had leaked for at least a year and necessitated the carrying of a can of water at all times. Remembering that Jeff had been the last to drive the old '49 Ford he climbed back out of the cab to check the jerry-can which was always kept in the bed. It aggravated him that the can, formerly a standard issue gas can that he had "requisitioned" from his jeep at the reserve unit, was near empty. Jeff was very negligent about such things but he had to admire his son's ability to work on cars. John filled the can with water adding a generous amount of Radiator Glycerin anti-freeze, in case it turned colder.

It wasn't a pretty day but promised to turn out fine if the sun could break through the thin high blanket of clouds. A typical Thanksgiving day for

Eastern Kentucky and perfect for a drive to the country.

He loafed along the twisty hilly roads in no particular hurry to get to Cotton's Turkey farm. The trip should take about an hour or so each way plus a half hour to select and have slaughtered the evening meal. Along about midway, on a stretch of two lane road that the county had failed to blacktop, the old faithful flathead quit. It sputtered a few times and a jab at the accelerator pedal caused a spurt of power but in a few turns of the tires it stopped, right smack in the middle of nowhere.

A cursory look at the engine showed no obvious signs of problems. He removed one of the small chrome racing style air cleaners and checked for fuel from the accelerator pump while he worked the throttle linkage by hand. Nothing. He was sure the gas tank was full as the gauge indicated about three-quarter. From the side of the road he broke the stalk of a now dried thistle, inserted it into the gas filler and confirmed this. Removing the fuel filter exposed the problem — dirt! Ten minutes and a few bars whistled of "As time goes by" and he was repositioning the cleaned sediment bowl oblivious to the car that had pulled up behind him.

"Having a little trouble, pal?" The rotund Sheriff demanded, adjusting his holster and gun, as he approached John.

"I think I've got it fixed now, officer," John replied, surprised to see this sloppily uniformed officer.

"You, ain't from around these parts, are you? What are you doin' here anyway? You got a partner off in the woods stealin' from some poor farmer or poachin' game?" The gun-toter accused.

"Why no sir. I...my truck just developed a dirty fuel filter and I was cleaning...."

"A likely story. We've been bothered by you non-residents coming out here to take what you can. Besides, it's against the law to park on the highway. I ought ta tow that heap of yours away and run you in just to make sure you ain't up to no good. But, seein' that it's Thanksgivin' an all, I'll just fine ya five dollars and let it go at that," the Sheriff ordered, an insincere, semi-toothless smile breaking out on his pudgy, unshaven face.

Catching the drift of the law officers intentions, John, now out from under the hood but careful not to make eye contact, replied in a humble tone, "Why thank you sir. I'll be out of here, lickety-split."

Closing the hood and sliding into the cab, John watched the Sheriff watch him, as the hood mounted red light oscillated slowly and ominously on the '55 Ford patrol car.

Drained of gas, the engine had to be cranked over many times in order for the fuel pump to refill the float bowls. It took more cranks than the old six-volt battery had in it. John was sure he was going to spend Thanksgiving in jail now.

The Sheriff approached the open truck window, curled his upper lip into a half smiled, and belched a putrid, rotted-tooth and whiskey, "Need a push, pal?"

Phew, maybe the cop, bad breath and misfeasance intentions aside, wasn't such a jerk after all. "It sure looks like it, sir. Mighty neighborly of ya to offer me your kind help."

"That's why the County put push bars on this here patrol car, so as we can be of service to the public. Course it'll cost ya a fiver," the obese badge carrier said with that same insincere sneer.

John produced another finn leaving him with less than ten dollars which he hoped was enough for the object of this trip — the bird.

With a tap and a push the little pick-up sprang to life. John waved a good-bye and gingerly drove away not knowing what the speed limit was and fearful of having to deal with the law again.

The Turkey farm was a pleasant experience if witnessing the slaughter of a live animal can ever be pleasant. But the men and women who did the work were nice enough. When he explained his tangle with the Sheriff, careful not to be too critical as any of them could be kin to the law man, they all expressed their understanding. They understood alright. This was their county and outsiders better mind their P's and Q's.

It was turning decidedly colder and giant dark, bulbous clouds now threatened snow. With a full radiator, topped off from his jerry-can, and the fresh bird carefully wrapped and on the seat next to him, John started for home. Mindful of the fact he had only a few dollars left — not enough for any more "fines" — he nonetheless increased his speed in hopes of beating the snow.

It was going to be a swell dinner. His brother, mom, dad and both of his boys would be there for this annual affair. He and Abigail, his wife, had spent the past weekend cleaning and polishing the little two bedroom frame house. It was their first home, bought with a G.I. loan in a new subdivision built just after the war for the returning soldiers. All the houses looked the same then, but as time passed and trees grew and new and different colored paint was applied the neighborhood took on the middle America look of any other period housing tract. Though he had expected to move to a bigger place they had grown used to the area and just stayed.

Uh-oh! Deep between mountainous hills, pulled to the side of the road, hood up, was the Sheriff's car. Too late to turn back on the narrow tree lined road, John hoped he could just slip on by with a wave of the hand. Slowing to a crawl, he double-clutched into first gear and racked his brain for a plausible story to tell of why he had to hurry on.

Abreast of the two tone brown sedan, the driver stepped in his path, hand raised — palm forward. Dangit now! "Howdy Sheriff. Hope everything is okay. I'd like to stop and talk, but I'm late for Thanksgiving dinner," John pleaded.

The Sheriff, his bulging eyes scanning the interior of John's cab stated, "Now that's no way to talk to a friend who just gave you a push and kept you out of jail. By the looks of that package on your seat I don't think they'll be startin' the dinner without you, will they?" Without waiting for an answer the man with the power of arrest continued. "It seems, ol' buddy, that my scout car has run out of gas and I just might have to declare an emergency and commandeer your truck so as I can get me some."

"Uh...sir. Why don't you radio for someone to come and get you?" John sheepishly tendered trying to be helpful without insulting the man.

"Can't. Radio won't reach from down in this hollar and besides, I'm the only one working in the whole county, this bein' a holly-day and all. So why don't...." The Man paused in his command to seize John's truck as he noticed the jerry-can in the bed of the pick-up. "Say, you wouldn't be tryin' ta hold out on me now, would-ja?"

"No, sir. What are you talking about?" John asked weighing his options. He could just race away and the fat cop would never be able to catch him or even radio for help. That idea was suppressed as he noticed the Sheriff casually massaging the big revolver on his hip.

"Is that can full — that one there in the back of this here truck?" The Sheriff asked, raising his voice as he reached over the side and shook the can.

"Sure is, Sheriff. Here let me help you, it's kind of dirty," John offered scrambling out of the cab. "I plumb forgot about my spare can. I always carry it with me just in case I get between stations.

"Now that's the right spirit. How much do you want for a few gallons? I don't want it all."

"Oh, I wouldn't charge you, being as you have helped me so much today. Besides, if I sold you the contents of this can that would be illegal since I don't have a vendors license. So if it's okay with you I'll just pour a few gallons into your tank and be on my way."

"Son, you catch on real quick. And just to show you I'm an alright guy I'm not going to notice that that olive-drab colored jerry-can has U.S. Government markings on it. And while I'm in a Thanksgiving spirit I'm gonna return that fiver you paid for the push awhile back. Course I can't return the fine for illegal parking — I'm sure you understand; that's County money."

It was a wonderful Thanksgiving. The turkey and trimmings, especially Abigail's pumpkin pie, were perfect. However, John, thankful as he was, felt a twinge of hypocritical guilt during the dinner prayer, but only a small one.

THE IDOL

Deep in the little boy
of all men fully grown,
lives the excitement for a
race engine's pure tone.

Some of the kids told the driver there was a lot of smoke coming from the back of the huge orange and cream colored bus, but he just kept right on driving like he didn't hear. This wasn't a "real" school bus with flashing lights and the words SCHOOL BUS in black on bright yellow paint like kids from other schools rode. We non-city residents were made to ride in giant black tired commercial buses that had shiny metal and glass fare boxes right up next to the driver. Of course, real school buses didn't have pictured advertisements over the top of the windows enticing the riders with such messages as: "Smoke Lucky Strike, LS/MFT" or "MUM - Takes the odor out of perspiration" or the boy with the funny hat shouting - "Call for Philip Morris". Kevin always wondered who Mr. Morris was but didn't dare ask, lest he show his ignorance. City buses, when transporting school children, were supposed to say SCHOOL BUS in the little window above the windshield. This day their bus said LOCKLAND, the driver obviously having forgotten to change it from his earlier city route.

Today was special and Kevin was in a hurry to get home. His idol, Sam, Sammy to his friends, was going to start up his race car. He liked Sammy because he always took time to explain things and, well, Sammy was just a neat guy. Even his name was cool, not some dippy name like, Kevin. He hated his name. To have a name like Sam or even Sammy told the world that he was tough and real cool. Nobody messed with guys named Sam. Guys with the name of Sammy just naturally knew about cars and engines and things. Kevin wanted to be everything that Sammy was, to do the things Sammy did, to build fast cars, drink beer, have a girl friend and do stuff that only cool men did. Well, maybe not the girl friend part.

Buses were slow and he wished his dad would

have sent the farm hand to pick him up. But the farm station wagon was only sent during bad weather when the buses weren't running. The farm wagon was neat because it was new and wasn't made of wood like the one the Kraft kids rode home in everyday. Though their wagon had the name of their farm in gold lettering on the doors, Kevin's had a two-way radio!

A few of the drivers allowed the kids to call them by their first names - something parents and teachers would never allow. But today's driver was not the regular man and didn't, or wouldn't, talk to any of the kids. Danny Roberts, who liked to tell everyone he lived on the outskirts of Glendale so it didn't sound like he lived on a farm, braved the smoke by sticking his head way out of the second from last window. No sooner than Danny was hanging out of the window, Kevin and Bruce holding onto him, a big bang and a giant ball of black smoke exploded from the back end of the bus. This got the attention of the driver who pulled over on the side of the road, pronto.

Kevin and Bruce trying to stay out of sight of the driver, who was now bulling his way down the isle, huddled on the steps to the rear door. Frantically trying to free his jacket from the window latch, Danny was caught in the act. The driver shaking his fist at the boys said, "you little whipper-snappers I'll warm your britches if you'ens broke ma bus". When he shook his fist, the money changer hanging from his belt, bounced so hard some coins jumped out scattering under and on the seats. He made a sixth grade girl pick them up while he went out to see what caused the smoke.

Kevin stood, embarrassed by the display of such a yellow streak - guys named Sam would never show fear. All the other kids were scared into silence, memories still fresh of the strapping a fifth grader had gotten by a bus driver only last month for saying a bad word. The boy had called a lady driver of a car that was next to the bus at a traffic light a, "damn old maid", because she ignored their warning that her 'Johnson Wire' was hanging down. Most ladies when told their 'Johnson Wire' was hanging would look worried and surprised and pull right over to check what was wrong and the kids would all howl with laughter.

Now they were going to be late and he might not get to see the starting of the engine. The race engine with two carburetors and Offen- something heads. For twelve years of age Kevin knew a lot about engines and cars and things. He had, with Sammy's help, made a jitney with an old lawn mower engine. It wouldn't go very fast and it didn't have a clutch but is was in fact a MOTOR VEHICLE. It was made with used wood scraps. He steered it with a rope and the front wheels were from his sister's baby carriage, but it was far better than riding a bike. To make a throttle; since time, money and maybe also expertise were short, Sammy had wired the butterfly valve wide open. A little dangerous, but with a kill switch mounted on the front cross bar, all the driver had to do to make it go was keep his foot on the momentary push-button/kill switch and lift his foot to slow down. The engine only operated under two conditions: wide open and off. Though Sammy had done most of the engineering, Kevin was proud of the braking system he developed and installed himself. He had used a cut down two-by-four on a pivot, that when pulled, caused the end hanging below the frame to scrape directly on the ground. It did help slow the jitney down some, but the best part was, by careful timing he learned to create full slides on the gravel driveway.

With smoke still pouring from the back of the bus, and some filtering its way inside, all the kids were made to get off and stand in the tall grass on the side of the road. Out in the country the grass, weeds and wildflowers grew high right up to the edge of the highway, not like in the city where everything look like a lawn. The wind had become gusty, bringing a slight chill to the scattered gang. Danny, Bruce and Kevin didn't dare untie their jackets from around their waist unless the girls put theirs on first. Fighting boredom, and maybe to keep warm, some of the kids started chanting:

"IKE, IKE HE'S OUR MAN,

THROW TRUMAN IN THE GARBAGE CAN.

IKE, IKE HE'S...."

The driver must have been for Mr. Truman because as soon as he got back from calling for another bus at a nearby farm he told them to pipe down. Nobody liked him very much but they all kept quiet, the memory of the fifth grader still fresh in everyone's mind.

Time, even to a sixth grader, can run as slowly as ninety-weight gear oil on a cold day. Waiting for the back-up bus, knowing that the first test ride of the coolest race car ever was soon to be history, ground the gears of Kevin's mind. Lost in dreams of stripped down jalopies tearing around well grazed pastured fields, towering clouds of dust rising from spinning tires and scattering livestock, Kevin played mind games envisioning Sammy - himself - at the wheel.

Idols, girls and careers come and go
as do words to a hit song,
but hot rodders needs for speed
are pure and forever life long

When the spare bus finally let him off at the junction of the state highway and Sharon Road it was beginning to get dark. The giant round blue Pure Oil sign was not lit and the station interior was dark. He had missed what was likely the most important event of Sharonville: the firing up of Sammy's rod. Surely everybody was there and would talk about it forever the way his uncles relived the barn raising over to the old Cutter place back in the thirties.

Dejected and angry he kicked a can in the direction of the farm as he zippered his jacket against the chill. He was a big kid now who had his own motor vehicle but the one mile walk home, down the country lane with the fenced pasture on one side and the deep woods on the other still caused him to keep to the fenced side even though he told himself he wasn't scared.

Less than half way, and before the silos were in view, he heard the distant roar of what he hoped was a full race V8 powered hot rod at open throttle - his idol's fenderless and hoodless thirty-six Ford roadster. The noise accompanied by a dark and low mass was soon visible coming out of the turn from Orchard Pike. The mass, amid billowing fogs of dust, dirt and gravel and sans any headlights, came right at the farm boy, now standing in the middle of the road.

Jumping to the fence row at the last possible moment Kevin shouted for his friend, who seeing the boy leap to safety, locked up the rear wheels just long enough to start the rod sliding on the gravel road. Within a few hundred feet Sammy had completed his square turn and was headed back to where Kevin stood. Above the din and dust came the magic words. Words that one born with a piston for a heart and gears for joints pine for: "Hi, kid. Wanna ride home?"

Fuel filled veins of a carburetor
or oil in the journals of a bearing,
is as blood is to the arteries of men
who live for speed and daring.

MY GIRL

Those of us
Weaned on rock & roll;
Have had it melded
To our very soul.

"Well...why don't you just go over and ask her out, man?" Chet chided.

"Ah, man. What if she puts me down. How 'bout if you ask her friend Bonnie to ask her if she'd go out with me," Terry pleaded to his buddy.

"Come-on, you chicken? The worst that'll happen is you'll end up the laughing stock of Crestview High," Chet rubbed it in.

"She sure is some good looking chick," Terry quietly dreamed out loud while sucking on the last of a Coke. "Some buddy you are."

Friday night, after the game, the place was packed. Terry was lucky and had found an "A-Bomb" stool, the red Naugahyde topped chrome pedestal type of bar stools that resembled the mushrooming bomb. Chet, standing next to his fellow sophomore and jostling for position with the throngs of other kids knocked loudly on the Formica counter top to attract the notice of the overburdened waitress. The knock caught Brittney's attention causing her to look directly at Terry. Instinctively and before he had time to flush he gave a quick smile then half turned to his pal with a look of contempt.

Brittney, seated in one of the red and white high-back booths, returned his ice breaker with shy downcasting of her soft blue eyes.

One of the football players, a large one, took another's letter sweater and began an impromptu game of keep-away. The white wool garment, emblazoned with a huge blue "C" on each pocket, was passed from student to student amid boisterous shouts of the gridiron players. Terry waited for the noise to subside, before inserting a dime into the counter top jukebox for Bobby Freeman's, *DO YOU WANNA DANCE*. Rehearsing what he was going to say while inspecting the pleats on his school slacks, Terry brushed his crew-cut with the palm of his hand and forced himself to start for the booth.

****

"Hey, Pete. I just came from inside and that Brittney chick is in there. She's in a booth over by the kitchen door," Alan advised, sliding into the passenger seat of the mildly customized '51 Chevy convertible.

"Yeah? Who's she with?" Pete asked, opening the door carefully so as not to knock the curb service tray that perched atop the partially raised window.

"She's not with anybody - just a bunch of girls. Before you go chasin' after that sweet young thing would you mind turning on the head lamps so as I can get a Coke or somethin'?"

Now standing outside the car, Pete had to reach through the open cozy wing to flip the custom light switch illuminating the chrome plated half-shielded and frenched head lights. "Turn 'em off when the car-hop comes - batteries ain't cheap."

"I dig ya, man," Alan said, slipping behind the wheel.

Pete was a Junior at rival Jackson Central High and had only briefly met the diminutive pony-tailed Brittney. It was a Crestview open house last week that he and a few of his fellow car club members, the High-Lifters, had crashed hoping to meet new chicks. She was wearing saddle shoes, a pink angora sweater and a heavy, dark, rust colored skirt, that stopped just above her white ankle socks. She wasn't what you'd call built, but she had bright red lips and great big light blue eyes that were always looking up from a downcast slightly cocked head. She had been dancing with two other girls and Pete just stepped between them, took her hand, spun her once, and as Jerry Lee Lewis's *GREAT BALLS OF FIRE* blasted from the speaker system, danced her into a corner.

To the Chantels, *MAYBE*, she told him, as they slow danced, she was 15, lived on Harpers Point, her mom was picking her up and she liked cool cars. He really wanted to go out with her not only because she was pretty in a cute sort of way, but it was cool to date chicks from Crestview.

Before they parted he told her to be at the Burger Boy on Friday night. He didn't ask her, he told her knowing it was best to establish who was in control. He had heard the car club's President expound on the importance of always keeping chicks in line and wanted to try out an older man's wisdom. She didn't say anything to his demand - but she didn't say she wouldn't. All she did was lower her head, tilt it a little, and look up at him with those huge eyes and a piston melting smile.

With the comb from the back pocket of his jeans, Pete smoothed his ducktail while walking toward the restaurant. A fellow rodder called from his '58 Bonny Tri-Power, with Olds Fiesta hubcaps, wanting to know if Pete was taking a date to the strip Sunday and did he want to double. Pete told him he'd let him know.

Before entering the restaurant, the Jac-Cen-Hi junior lit a fresh Camel from the pack in the pocket of his club jacket. Some of the guys always kept their fags rolled up in their T-shirts sleeves, but Pete thought that was uncool, especially if you're trying to make it with a chick. In the reflection in the plate glass front windows he could see his rod. It had taken all of his money from his part time job and most of his time but it was worth it if chicks dug it. He had installed lowering blocks on the rear, nosed and decked the hood and trunk, frenched the head and tail lights, removed the outside door handles and rigged solenoids under the front fender to operate the doors. The car was still in primer but he had drawn the outlines for the flame job he was planning to do after another pay day or two. The interior was rolled and pleated, black corduroy with pink accent panels. Someday he was going to chop the top and slip an Olds Rocket "88" under the hood.

Inside the rowdy Burger Boy the Harry-high-schoolers crowded Pete into Terry as both boys, oblivious to each others intentions, headed in the same direction.

Terry arrived ahead of his competition, but Brittney recognized Pete first with an, I'm-glad-to-see-you-smile, and a bat-of-the-eye-lashes.

With Bobby Freeman pleading on the loud speakers, Terry, trying to act cool by shaking his shoulders and squinting his eyes to mimic the crooner, whispered, "Do ya wanna dance?"

Brittney, giggled, looked to her girl friends for support then to Pete for an instant before taking another sip on her Cherry Coke. Terry, still mocking the vocalist of the jukebox, began to feel a little silly, but nonetheless, mouthed the request a second time, ready to bop on out of there if she ignored him again.

"Dance? Here?" The pert blonde asked looking up from those robin's egg blues.

Straightening up and folding his arms in order to flex his biceps, Terry continued, "Well, if you want to Miss Cohen. But I was really hoping I might take you to the Phi Ep sock hop tomorrow night and dance with you there."

Pete, suddenly realizing that this songster, this impostor, was trying to cut his time, half shouted. "Hey Brittney, come outside a minute, I want to talk to ya."

Another sip of the virgin Coke, a few giggles and glances to compatriots, Brittney, keeping her head down, looked up out of the corner of her eye at Pete, "Please, I'm having a Coke with my friends. Why don't you come back later...Peter."

Pete, ruffled at being rebuked, sized up the kid standing next to him with a look of disdain. Though the kid was a little beefier he was about the same height. Pete shoved him, but not too hard, saying, "Stay away from my girl, pal. Beat it."

Terry, with two years of gym team competition under his belt, felt his muscles harden. Though he had never been in a fight he was reasonably sure of himself. Without looking at his attacker he intoned, "Watch who you're shovin', PAL." The word pal was spit out with emphasis but not too much acid; he really didn't want to fight.

Pete, also not actually looking for a fistfight, looked to Brittney saying, "I'll be in my rod. So whenever you're finished with your Coke come on out. But, I ain't waitin' forever, baby." To Terry, he leaned closer, surprised to get a whiff of Sportsman D-Bar, the same deodorant he used, "I mean what I said, pal."

Terry balled his fists and turned to face this threat as Pete pivoted toward the door. The girls giggled. The closer Pete got to the door the more Terry's chest puffed up. Finally, confident the threat had passed, he resumed his attention for the favor of the perky teenager.

Miss Brittney Cohen, feigning indifference to the dangerous conditions that had almost been brought to a head on her account, huddled with her booth mates giggling and talking in whispers.

Confidence, overloading his normally bashful demeanor, allowed Terry to again ask, and in a louder voice, "Excuse me. Could I take you to the hop tomorrow night? I'd really like to...Brittney" The last sentence said a little softer.

"Oh yes, I'd love to go. But, I'd like to know who I'm going with. I've seen you at school but I don't know your name. Are you in the Fraternity?" she asked, sweet as cream.

With visions of ecstasy flashing through his mind and adrenaline surging through his body Terry stammered, "I'm sorry, I'm, I'm Terry Motch and yes I'm in Phi Ep - well I'm not actually in the fraternity yet, but, I am going to rush Phi Ep. If you give me your phone number I'll call you tomorrow morning and let you know what time I'll pick you up."

Wow! He could hardly believe it. He had stolen the best lookin' chick in the place right from under the nose of a leather-jacket-wearin', ducktailed hot rodder. His girl my eye! Nevertheless, Terry, not wishing to push his luck, hopped into his stock '53 Chevy and cut out.

Pete, angry at the way things turned out and mystified as to what a chick like Brittney could possibly see in that other cat, sulked for a few minutes...until the young lady with the pony tail and the shy blue eyes settled into the black rolled and pleated corduroy.

We builders of hot rod cars,

With twin carbs and dual exhaust,

Know true, true love better,

Than all others on which it is lost.

TRAIN RUN

He drove a hot rod Ford
That could lay a fat black patch.
That punk was a fool
Whose daring had no match.

Bonnie Sue knew, deep down, that he wasn't a
"bad kid", but some of her friends and especially her
mom didn't see it that way. Tommy, she felt, was just
frustrated, though she wasn't sure what it was that he
was so antsy about. He didn't do well in school, but
he was very smart. He had, after all, figured out,
without any help, how to take his car motor all apart
and put it back together again. Besides, he had said
he loved her. True, it was only once and in a fit of
passion. It was on a Friday night, last month, at the
drive-in. It was one of those, Francis the talking mule
flicks. The movie was boring so they just made out.
Tommy kept trying to touch her where she didn't
think he should. They fought, she cried, and Tommy
said, "I really love you, Bonnie Sue, I mean it."

Bonnie Sue was sure that if only they could both
finish school, get married (and Tommy in a good job)
she'd be able to change his fast driving ways and
other things that might need adjustments. Right now
all she wanted was for Tommy to be here.

Tommy, at 16 and a half, was one of the more
dedicated and speed crazed hot rodders in his
sophomore class. Though he had never applied to
one of the hot rod clubs for membership he was
always thinking about joining - if they would take
him. That was the rub. He'd already had two tickets

for speeding and he had a reputation for fast driving on city streets. Hot rod clubs frowned on "squirrels", as they called them. He had never shied away from a traffic light race even when Bonnie Sue pouted about his high speed drags. Trouble was, he couldn't figure her out. She was pretty enough but she was always talking about love and all that mushy stuff and she only sometimes seemed to enjoy the drag racing - legal or otherwise. On their first few dates she had been all excited about his races even going so far as to taunt one of her girl friends because this friend's steady drove a stocker.

But he was really burned up that she had so little regard for the fact that he held the record for the Train Run and now must defend that honor. Johnny Medford, with his Daddy's brand new '55 Olds 88, had bested Tommy's record by at least 50 yards. For Tommy to let this go unchallenged would be like wearing your sister's bloomers or something equally unthinkable.

The troubles with Bonnie Sue culminated last night as they sat sipping Cokes in the lot of the West Chester Pike Bun Boy. Removing his arm from her shoulders to light a Lucky, Tommy asked while trying to make it sound like a casual mention, "You want to ride with me when I go for the Train Run record tomorrow night?"

"Oh, Tommy, you're not going to do that again are you?" Not waiting for an answer she continued while tossing her pony tailed head in a dignified affront, "Tommy, I swear you're going to kill yourself one of these days with all this crazy...."

"Come on Baby I just have ta do it, ya dig. I'm not gonna to be no chicken hearted punk. I'll be the coolest cat in town if I beat that harry-high-schooler in his daddy's stocker."

"Oh Tommy, it's so dangerous I just worry that you'll be killed and I won't have you. I think you're the coolest guy at North Anderson anyway. Winning The Run can't make you any better in my eyes. Please, just for me don't do it," Bonnie Sue pleaded, all pouty faced.

"Aw, don't cry honey. I know you dig me and all, but this is something I just have to do. Besides it should be a snap. The last time I ended up backing off before the tracks, I had so much reserve power. And since then I've added dual points. And, hey, I'll put in new plugs in the morning to be extra safe! Don't worry," Tommy boasted, flicking his butt over the trunk of the flopped top of the faded black '51 Ford.

The object of his non-romantic desires, the '51, sported two-deuces with chrome racing air cleaners and glass-packed dual exhaust. It was not only fast but it sounded cool. In addition to the Mallory distributor he had recently added he was planning to install Offenhauser high compression heads and maybe a Clay-Smith cam. His after school job at Wylie's Pure Oil Station didn't allow for many luxuries even though he was top paid of all the part timers at $1.10 per hour.

The rest of the evening was like, no-wheres-ville. They ended up, as they always did after a date, parked at the old abandoned army base down near the feed mill. Every time he tried to put the move on Bonnie Sue she'd scrunch up closer to her door and whimper about how she just wasn't in the mood. Chicks! Who could understand them? What kind of mood could she be in parked in a lover's lane? He took her straight home, not even walking her to door. Then he pealed out because he knew it would make her angry.

Saturday, Train Run day, was chilly for a September day in Texas. Tommy, had managed to install the new plugs between pumping gas and oil changes at Wylie's service station. The powerful flathead was running cherry and sounding very sweet. The soon-to-be nosed and decked rod had even gotten a wax job compliments of the kids who hung out at the station. Kids, of course meant anyone who wasn't old enough to have a drivers license. These kids, in hopes of being able to get a ride to the race area would do almost anything for the privilege of seeing one of their idols in a run against death.

Just before quitting time, Johnny, riding in Delbert's straight eight Pontiac because his dad had stripped him of his driving rights upon finding out about the Train Run, stopped in at Wylie's.

"Hey Mr. Cool, I hear tell that you're gonna try to beat my record tonight?" Johnny sneered.

"Yeah, that's right sonny and I'll do it in a rod I built myself, not in my daddies stocker," Tommy shot right back in a menacing tone.

"Why, I ought to climb out of here and...."

"Okay, Okay, punks. Enough of this tough guy talk. Do you guys wanna belly-ache or race," Delbert demanded, taking control of the pre- race details. "Now listen up: me and Harry as witnesses, plus about a dozen kids, watched Johnny here, beat the train from the no passing sign through the intersection. Now if you want to beat this record you must start at the end of the guard rail. Ya dig, Tommy?"

"Well, I was thinking about starting halfway between the sign and the rail and...."

"No, no that won't do. You have to use a permanent fixture, dig. Otherwise cats would be claiming to have started at all kinds of locations and the record would be muddied. We talked about it and that's the way it has to be. So, unless you're yellow we'll see ya five minutes before the eight-three-eight," Delbert stated.

Curling his lip, Tommy spat, "I ain't yella - I'll be there."

He didn't have time to be nervous only time to shower, change clothes and chow down with his mom and sister before heading for Bonnie Sue's.

She wouldn't get into the car unless Tommy promised not to race the train, almost tearfully pleading - promising "anything" if he wouldn't make

The Run. Too late. Even the thought of "anything" with Bonnie Sue didn't change his mind, though for a moment or two he had his doubts.

Tires squealing and defiance in his eyes
With his girl he had a fight
he cut out for the showdown as she cried,
"I know I'll grieve if you race this race tonight"

They were waiting for him, a dozen or so classmates, buddies and kids all lined up on the grass strip that lay between the road and the tracks of the mainline. Some of the kids, seeing the empty passenger seat, offered or begged to ride shotgun for this run for the record.

By 8:47 no sound akin to a train had been heard - the eight-three- eight was late! However, all was well and tension was relieved within a few minutes as the sound of the eight-three-eight, out of Wichita Falls, pierced the cool evening air. Without any discussion two of the spectator cars pulled onto the concrete blocking the highway so that no other vehicles could get in the way. Tommy moved the '51 to the point adjacent with the end of the guard rail, rapped the accelerator a few times and stared down the straight-away.

A little over a mile away the slightly curving tracks met and crossed the highway. All he had to do was beat the train to this point and he would again be top rodder at North Anderson High and surely Bonnie Sue's faith in his abilities would be returned.

The plume of thick gray smoke could be seen superimposed on the clear twilight sky from over a mile away and long before the west bound express itself was visible. Tommy raced the engine again and again wishing he had a tach to more accurately gauge the speed of his mill. Some of the kids were jumping up and down with excitement. Delbert stood slack jawed and Johnny sat, wide eyed, glad it wasn't him this time.

The importance of the lateness of the eight-three-eight didn't register with Tommy as he readied himself for a good clean start. Glancing over his shoulder to the tracks he timed the dumping of the clutch to the exact moment the locomotive was even with him and the guard rail. The huge 4-8-4 iron monster, oblivious to its place in the destiny of that night, overshadowed the gathering of children playing with their toys.

Tires spinning, the little flathead strained in first gear, as the train roared by. A speed shift to second brought a chirp of rubber and Tommy felt a twinge of pride as the force of acceleration pushed him into the seat back. Just when it seemed that the engine was about to explode he power shifted into third. Now topping 70 miles per hour he dared a glance at the rushing sound to his right - the sound of a death knell?

Tommy was horrified to see that he was just now beginning to pass the speeding train. He was sure he should have been equal to the engine by now, but he was at least one car plus the tender behind. He pushed harder on the gas pedal and strained to hear if his engine had a miss or something. 90, 95, the needle swept past the 100 MPH mark and still he was not in front. The convergence, the intersection of death, was dead ahead. Where was the miscalculation? Did someone move the guard rail? Was the train running faster than its usual 60 MPH?

Yeah! that's it. The train was late so they're running faster to make up for lost time. Flashing through his jumbled mind were thoughts of clamping on the binders and turning into the double barbed wire fence to his left - taunts of chicken - yellow - Bonnie Sue....

He slammed the massive locomotive
that was doin' better than 70 per
and when they pulled him from the carnage
his last thoughts were of her.

DAYDREAMS

Everyone has dreams and schemes.
Some only build castles in the air,
Others skimp and save and plan;
While a few live reality with a flair

Maybe, just maybe, if I hadn't chased that fly ball so hard. After all it was only a scratch game and it was only the second out, if only....

"Mom...Mom what time's dinner? I'm starving," Stan wailed, frustrated that thoughts of *'that game'* had disrupted the building of his rod.

"Now Stanley," she always called him by his formal name even though he begged her not to, especially not in front of any of the guys. "Just be patient son it will be ready in a jiffy."

Building the rod had been difficult today. Every time he tried to work out final gear to tire size ratios his mind would wander. Sometimes he wouldn't fight it and just let the memories and fantasies take him on a trip. Most of the morning had been spent thinking about Annette.

Nothing, absolutely nothing could be greater than a ride through the Burger Boy lot with Annette sitting next to him in this, the finest machine Rockville would ever see. Trouble was he not only had to actually finish the task of building, get a license, win her love and....he didn't want to think about the...*and*.

Sometimes it seemed the jobs at hand were insurmountable. But, boy, oh boy if he could pull it off he would be the coolest cat at Thomas Jefferson High. Of course the Rod Busters and maybe even the Piston Poppers would offer him a coveted membership in their clubs.

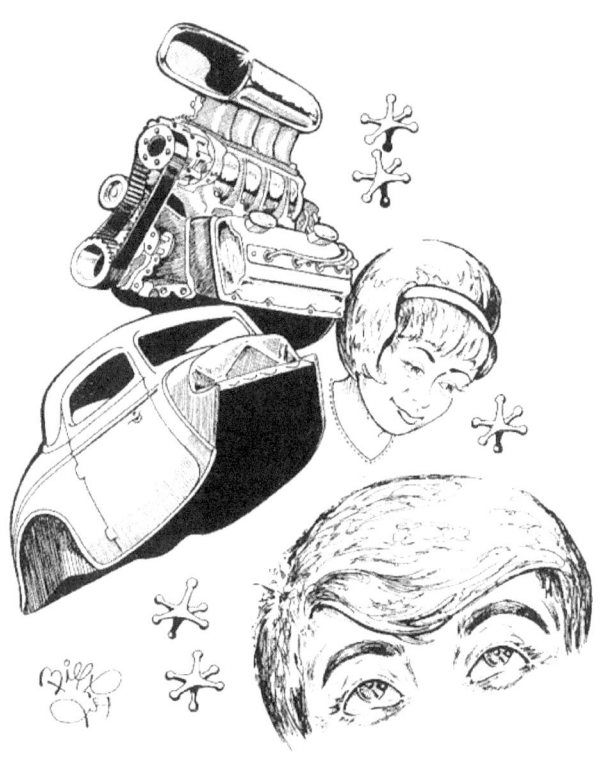

He had palled around with Stu and Tom, both of which had Rod Busters plaques dangling from the backs of their cars. Tom had even taken him to the strip a few times in his Jimmy six-banger powered '34 Plymouth. Tom had almost always pulled trophy in D/Altered Coupe but had yet to win in C/AC, forced to the higher class after installation of a roots blower.

Stan wouldn't make the mistake of just slapping a blower on a carbureted engine. He'd use a 6-71 huffer with Hilborn fuel injection. He would build for A/AC class and that way he could utilize the full potential of his 392 Chrysler Hemi. He had toyed with the idea of building a special tube frame but really didn't think he knew enough about welding and suspension systems to attempt it. Instead he believed that weight could be saved with careful body modification and drilling holes in all nonessential components. In addition he'd do away with the fenders and running boards, sectioned body and a radical 4" top chop. On the inside he'd design two sets of interchangeable seats and removable door panels. For the strip he'd have one ultra light bucket and no door inserts. But, when he took his best girl out or maybe entered it into a car show he'd have a rolled and pleated naugahyde bench seat, so she could sit next to him, between the matching door panels. Yes sir it would be some '34 Ford - fastest and best engineered in the county - the envy of all, even Annette.

The first time he saw her he was smitten but knew it wouldn't be cool to let on. She was a year younger and friends with his sister. They were only kids then. They were playing jacks on the kitchen floor one rainy day a few years ago. Annette had just moved next door and right away became best of friends with little sister Judy. He allowed them to taunt him into a game just so he could get to know her. He wasn't very good and hated to be shown up by his sister but he played anyway. He went out on fivezes.

Stan laughed to himself reminiscent of his early daydreams...of how he'd win her love by rushing into her fully inflamed house to save her. How he'd carry her unconscious body out of the burning building, covering her face with his as flames seared his arms and back. Of how he'd dive into the frozen water to rescue her after she had fallen through the ice on Miller's pond. Yeah, those were kids thoughts. It never happened in real life, but winning the regional trophy, or even Top Eliminator, at the drag strip was a sure way to impress a chick such as Annette. And that wasn't kid stuff.

He knew how it would happen, but he'd wait for the proper time when the rod was finished. She'd stop by the garage, like she does when looking for Judy, and he'd show her some of the innovations he had made on the rod. She'd be impressed as always and then he would say something cool, like, "You're a real cool chick and I'd like..." No he couldn't use any cool cat talk. He'd have to be straight and use words that a mature man, a man who can build cars, would use. "Miss Margolis, I'd be most honored...." Naw, man, too formal. Well he had lots of time to work on it. One thing sure he would have to rehearse it. He didn't want to say something dumb like he did the time he asked Sally Truesdale to dance.

Time to stop thinking and work on the rod. The rear end would be a 9-inch Ford truck with 4.56 gears turning M&H slicks mounted on either 14 or 15 inch mag wheels. All this was going to cost a ton but with the money he had saved from four years as a newspaper boy plus what he'd be earning at Toliver's Cities Service gas station he'd be able to swing it. Old man Toliver had always told him that he could have a job as soon as he was old enough. Yeah, all the details were taken care of all except....

"Stanley, it's time for dinner. It's matzo ball soup from the nice Jewish lady at the bakery. She made it this morning because she knows you like it," his mother said running her fingers through her son's crop of dusty-red hair. Stan said a silent Hail Mary as he prepared to eat the Kosher food everyone, except him, seemed to like.

Admiring his mother's brilliant blue shirt-waist dress, accented with a white sash tied tightly around her waist, gave Stanley an idea about the color his rod would be. Women were always better with color combinations. He'd paint the coupe whatever color Annette thought best. That would be a perfect way to break the ice with her. If she thought she was contributing to the beast then it would only be natural that she would not only want to ride in it but would surely have great admiration for him for trusting her judgment! This revelation caused him to almost choke on the soup as he hurried to finish eating so he could get back to building. Now he wouldn't have to wait for the perfect moment to ask this pretty miss for a date. He'd just make her sort of a partner in the project and let things happen naturally. Stan, ol' boy, you're a genius.

Race day dawned bright and sunny the kind of clear day that follows the passing of a cool front. All the hard work was now on the line. If he lost today it wouldn't be the end of the world but surely it would cost him status. Of course, if he didn't race then they would never know if Blue Bird, that's what Annette named the coupe, was as fast as it looked. But then again, the guys would also think he was chicken or the rod was for show only. He built it to run and run it would. If he didn't pull trophy he'd keep at it until he had the fastest in his class.

The first run during the time trials produced a very quick 104.6, the fastest time of the morning. His elimination runs pitted him against only one other in-class rod, a '40 Willy's with a blown Caddy engine. The Willy's was no problem and for the trophy run he dusted off a '32 five- window Ford housing a Hemi like his.

Annette, excited by all the attention, noise and commotion hung on his arm every minute that he wasn't strapped into the midnight blue rod. When it came for the top eliminator run he wound up facing a B/Dragster complete with parachute. The dragster had clocked 121+ in the early rounds and it looked like a lost cause. Still, he had to be happy that he had made it all the way to the final race of the day. His toil of labor and love had brought him to this moment, facing the fastest of the fast - and with his best girl at his side.

At the starting line he rapped the perforated aluminum accelerator pedal a few times to clear the plugs and felt the power of this custom machine strain at the clutch. To force his concentration he had to fight to suppress his swelling pride - his arrogance of knowing that every nut, bolt, valve and gear was by his hand and ingenuity alone.

Now it was a matter of nerves. He could beat the mighty dragster - he had to. Not for Annette or to excite the spectators but just for himself - for overcoming the odds - the seemingly insurmountable odds.

At the same instant the starter dropped the flag, Stan's left Keds covered appendage dumped the clutch while his practiced right foot feathered the gas. With just enough power to keep the huge ten inch slicks in a controlled spin the little Altered Coupe shot toward the finish line, a scant 440 yards away.

Out of the corner of his eye he could see billows of smoke as the rails next to him over powered. Seconds that seemed to last forever ticked by as the Stewart Warner tach swept toward redline, slam, he hit third gear and dared a glance to the next lane fearing the B/Dragster had recovered from his spin-out and would be coming by. It was not there! Wow! He had beat the best. The giant three foot tall trophy would be his. Oh, Annette, we did it - I love you!

Achoo. It was the sneeze that brought him back to reality. "Mom. I need a little help, please."

"What's wrong honey."

"I sneezed and need a wipe, please. Mom, do you think if I hadn't gone after that fly ball so hard that all this wouldn't have happened?"

"Now Stanley, the doctors have said that playing hard doesn't cause polio. Now stop thinking and worrying about things you can't change. Try thinking about what you're going to do when you're well," she said, wiping his nose. "You won't have to stay in this iron lung for ever."

Author's Note: Polio, a disease of the central nervous system, was epidemic among children in the 1950s. It affected different persons in different ways, some only lost the use of a limb, others, such as Stanley in the above story, could only survive in an iron lung. The iron lung, though a miracle inasmuch as it forced a paralyzed diaphragm to function, usually did not extend life beyond a few years.

THE HERO

He hadn't been back to his old home town in over twenty years and then it was only for a funeral. The rolling hills of the asphalt interstate looked like the flat side of a giant blower belt cut and thrown casually across the beautiful south central Ohio farm land. He laughed to himself at his unintentional play on words; a blower belt draped around the "farm belt" of the nation. Crossing the county line, his county line, brought a flood of memories. Memories of fun, simpler times and the race, the race for life. Where was it — the spot where the old road had been sliced by this modern highway?

Daydreaming was brought to a rapid halt by the sound of a siren attached to blue and red flashing lights. A quick glance at the speedometer confirmed his suspicions that it was he, for whom the sirens tolled. Swell. Welcome home hero. That's what you get for getting all melancholy while piloting a high powered sports car.

Down shifting his fully restored seventy-four, 454, Corvette he pulled to the side of the road adjacent to what appeared to be the remnants of an old two lane highway. The narrow strip of weed-sprouting black-top was now nothing more than a very long driveway for what looked like the south field to the Mulhouser farm. He wondered if any of the same family farmed it now.

"I've stopped you for exceeding the posted speed limit, sir. May I please see your operator's license," the Deputy Sheriff monotoned.

65

"I'm sorry officer. I guess I wasn't paying attention," he stated truthfully while searching his wallet — hoping that the license hadn't expired. "Is that the Mulhouser farm over there?" Nodding toward the fields of soybean, the Vette driver asked.

"Used to be. Fellah by the name of Krantz, from up around Columbus, owns it along with about three other farms around here. Absentee owner. Has a

family by the name of, of...it'll come to me in a minute, tenant farming it now."

Handing the license to the officer he noted a slight pot belly contained by a sharply creased and neat shirt. This smart looking uniform was embellished with the standard polished brass accompaniments plus gold sergeant stripes. The deputy looked to be in his thirties though his graying hair could place him closer to forty. The neatly lettered name tag, Sgt. Vogt, jarred him. Might be, but Vogt was a common name in this area.

"You from these parts, Mr. Sampson?"

"I was born and raised not far from the old Mulhouser place. Lived here till I went away to college. First time I've been back in twenty years," the Corvette man said. Remembrances of a young, dying mother bounced around in the combustion chambers of his mind like a broken connecting rod in a V8 engine — jagged edges tearing away pieces of the past.

He had been called a hero by some and a crazy fool by others. The county newspaper covered the incident with only a one quarter column saying they were afraid that publicity of that kind would only encourage others to ignore proper procedures.

After graduating from high school he had worked that summer, the summer of fifty-seven, on the Keaton farm. He, and the rest of the farm hands, had just taken a lunch break when the young and very pregnant kitchen helper, white as a sheet and holding a towel under her tummy, stumbled into the mud room.

Returning the driver's license the deputy asked, "Sampson. Seems I should know that name. You have any kin here?"

Blinking his eyes to snap back to the present he responded slowly, "Not any more. I was an only child, my mother died in seventy-two. My father lives with me."

"I'm not going to cite you, but I am going to run your VIN number through our computer," the officer said in his official tone as he copied the VIN on his note pad. It'll only take a second or two if the system's up.

As the deputy turned toward his cruiser, Carl Sampson turned to the old stretch of blacktop and back four decades. "Help, please! I fell. I think I'm hemorrhaging!" The mother-to-be gasped as she surged into the kitchen. It only took Mr. Keaton a few seconds to sum up the situation. Knowing that the volunteer ambulance was at least 20 minutes away and the ride to the nearest hospital was over half an hour farther he looked to his young summer helper, "Son, will that hot rod of yours make it to the County Hospital over to Skeetersville any faster than ma old wagon?" The calmness of his employer strengthened him as he shook his head up and down stammering, "Yes sir, Yes sir."

"Well, bring it up here to the back door while the missus and I carry her out. The "missus", blood up to her elbows, was stuffing another towel between the neighbor's wife's legs all the while cooing a soothing message of all's well.

He remembered running to his rod with the only thought in his mind, did he have enough gas for a mercy run to the county seat in the next county over. He'd spent the past year building his pride and joy — a 1935 Ford, three-window coupe. He had, with the help of various hot rod magazine articles, chopped the top, channeled the body, dropped the front axle, installed a LaSalle transmission and hopped up a swapped engine.

He'd done his work well. The full race flat-head fired on the first crank of the starter. Twin pipes, rumbling through Glass-pacs, boosted his confidence as he slipped the tires gently across the gravel barn yard.

There was barely enough room for two, much less a pregnant woman in the altered coupe's tiny interior. As the missus packed towels, Mr. Keaton gripped his arm and in a low steady voice intoned, "Son, she may not pull through, but there's a chance you can save the baby. But you've got to step on it. I'll call over to the hospital and tell 'em you're ah comin'."

He spun gravel all the way to the blacktop, turned east and got on it hard getting just a piece of third gear before having to shut down for the first set of 'S' bends. Today, he realized, would be the test of his handiwork as he set the little coupe into the first sweeping turn. At the apex, inside front tire on the dirt berm, he poured the coal to the mighty Mercury flathead. The rear tires howled in protest as the power curve of the Clay-Smith cam let in all the fuel the over-sized pistons could suck through the polished ports.

There was no traffic and he used all the roadway he dared. For the next few minutes his concentration was so intense that he hadn't had time to check his gauges much less the condition of his passenger. Just ahead loomed the narrow chicane, the right followed by a hard left at the Mulhouser farm, that led to the only section of completed interstate in Spartan County. There he would have a chance to check everything.

Tires baying in dissent, young Carl brought his primer-red rod down to just under thirty-five from well above seventy for the first bend. He powered out of the final curve, tires squealing and engine screaming, to catch a glimpse of old mister Mulhouser out of the corner of his eye. The third generation farmer displayed his disgust at the speeding hot rod by shaking his fist at Carl from atop his John Deere.

Within minutes he was slamming the gear shift into third for the longest straight stretch of the run. Pleased at the sound of the three Stromberg ninety-sevens whooshing air through wide open butterflies he took the time to check the gauges. Oil, eighty pounds; temp, almost 200; fuel, cresting the empty mark; tach, 4200 and climbing slowly; speedometer, mounting steadily at 105. He looked to the little lady. Clutching her blood soaked towels, she forced a cringing smile that mocked her vacant stare.

One hundred and fifteen — one-twenty — one-twenty-two. The steering felt light and there was a pronounced vibration. He backed down to just under 120 and the vibration slackened. Water temp hovering at 210, he passed the new green sign: Skeetersville Exit — 5 miles. He was over half way there but, even at 120 miles per hour it felt extremely slow — time wise. Every time he tried to go above 122 the vibration increased alarmingly. It must be those old wire wheels. He'd hand tightened each spoke and wire brushed them down to bare metal but still, true run-out was difficult to attain on those old wheels. He wished he'd had the money to buy new chrome-plated Dayton Wires or polished mags.

Drivers of the few cars he passed, at over twice their speed, stared wide-eyed and slack jawed at him. None tried to race him.

Slowing for the end of the divided highway gave him a final chance to study the interior. All okay except the temperature gauge. Maybe he had blown a head gasket which could, at these speeds, seize his perfectly rebuilt engine in short order. No question though, he would have to keep it floored.

After the zig-zag he ran a short straight tight in second gear and then had to double clutch down into first for the hairpin leading to the final set of 'S' bends. A quick glance at his passenger brought terror to his already over excited mind. Her head was listing at an unnatural angle, tongue visible and eyes half closed. He dared to take his hand from the wheel to shake her. "Lady. Lady," he screamed over the din of the high revving engine as he shook her near wrist. The entire arm flopped like an old heater hose. They were now down to minutes. He pushed the little copper wheeled coupe to its limit at each turn heading into the final straight. Here he'd have to open her up all the way, damn the temperature! Damn the vibration!

The newspaper reported that from the time the call was logged at the hospital to the minute the fenderless hot rod, smoke pouring from its hoodless engine, screeched to a halt at the back door of the emergency room only seventeen minutes had lapsed. The reporter believed it to be a mistake but, young tow-headed Carl Sampson, knew better. The account further noted that Mrs. Vogt died in surgery but the premature baby boy was saved. The Vogt family called him a hero and named the boy James Carl in his honor. The doctor unequivocally stated that had they arrived only a few minutes later the child would not have survived. Contrarily, the police chief admonished his deed threatening to take him to jail if he ever did it again.

****

Sergeant Vogt jarred him into the present with the news that his Vette wasn't on the NCIC hot list. He had broken into a damp sweat, not for fear of the car being stolen, but from reliving the old memories.

Clearing his throat, "Say...ah, Sergeant, is your name, by any chance, James Carl Vogt?"

"Why no, but my little brother was James Carl. How could you know him?"

"Well, ah, I sort of met him once. Knew his mother too, but it was a long time ago. What-ever became of him?"

The officer stroked his chin while eyeing this stranger who was inquiring about his brother and a mother he never knew. "James Carl was a volunteer firefighter. He died a little over two years ago, saving a child from a burning building. Now how could you possibly know my mothe...OH MAN! The name didn't register until just now. Why, why, you're the kid...the hero, who drove a hot rod Ford from the old Keaton place to Skeetersville in seventeen minutes to save his life. Let me shake your hand Mr. CARL Sampson and say thanks, thanks very much."

Uncomfortable as it was, Carl twisted in his seat extending his hand for the obligatory grasp.

"I'm sorry to learn of your brother's death...." After the brief awkward silence that imprisoned the grown men in their own revelations, Carl continued, "Whatever happened to the Keaton's, and that police chief and do you know what became of my coupe?"

"The last I saw of your car...say, it's almost my quitting time. Why don't you come on over to the house and we can catch you up on all these things. I'm sure my brother's family would like to meet you.

AMERICA

Those few words, on the corn dust colored telegram, informing Bucky of his canceled liberty, had just about ruined all plans for his fourth-of-July weekend celebration. Bucky, a nickname earned for staying on a not-too-tame horse at age six, and not for his slight overbite, was all set to spend the four day weekend with Katy. Man, it just wasn't fair!

He knew the possibility of a shortened furlough and had taken the chance when a hop had become available to Chicago. It had been only a few days since he had thumbed from O'Hare to his parents home in Emporia. Now all he had left was one day - one day in which to spend more time with his girl, ready his '55 and catch a few hours of shut-eye. Then it was 30 hours to the base, if he pushed it. He had decided on his last liberty that he wanted his car on base with him.

Also parked in the detached garage behind the white frame house was a gift from his Uncle Bill, a partially disassembled '34 Chevy Town Coach. Uncle Bill abandoned it to him when the clutch went out. Uncle Bill was really his Great Uncle who preferred his horsepower one or two at a time - as in front of a carriage. The clutch gave out because first gear was stripped and Uncle Bill thought it wouldn't hurt to just forgo first and start slowly in second gear. But drive train didn't matter because he planned to use the engine and transmission he had salvaged from his Dad's wrecked Caddy. Just as soon as his tour was complete he was going to transform that rusty old trunkless Chevy into the coolest hot rod Emporia would ever see.

The '55 Chev had been the first thing he attended to upon arriving home. He had hoped to have time to install a Corvette solid lifter cam to compliment the two-fours he had bolted on last year. He already had the 097 cam, so if he took it with him maybe he could find a place to work on it during off time while on shore duty.

It only took a jump start and air in two of the tires to put the mildly customized rod back into action. The second thing he had done was to visit Katy. She had been his girl since junior high when he had fought Stevie Bilkus after Stevie called her a stuck up old maid. He hadn't really wanted to win her over then; it was more a matter of exercising an excuse to whip Stevie.

Katy had gotten a job with the telephone exchange after graduation and had promised to wait for his enlistment to end so they could get married. Buck, that's what he called himself, though no one else did, except Katy, wasn't sure he wanted to get married so soon. Not that Katy wouldn't make a fine wife, its just that, well, he still had cars to build, places to go, wild oats to sow and you know, other stuff to do. Of course, if he let her get away she'd be hard to replace - she could have been a Breck girl. Katy had volumes of smooth silky blond hair that wound around her head and neck in giant curls like the chrome bumper on a '57 Olds. Besides her cover-girl good looks, she could cook! Meat loaf stuffed with hard boiled egg and mashed potatoes with thick gravy were her specialty - and his favorite.

The first set of fireworks, those put on by the local Chamber of Commerce at the high school ball field (the field where he had played two years as second string linebacker and Katy had been a cheerleader) was the best he'd seen the town do. It was fun, and comforting too, squeezing into the packed bleachers with so many long time familiar old classmates, neighbors and friends.

The second set of "fireworks" topped the first set by a mile. Katy had wrapped herself around him the minute the '55 had settled in at the local passion pit. Her softness and passion was only tempered by her tenacious reluctance to "go all the way". He thought that since a war was always possible and he could get killed she should show her love and devotion. No soap. He had tried that line before joining the Navy, but she was just as adamant now as then - not before marriage - period! Not that he was a virgin or anything, his shipmates had taken care of that at a brothel at Subic Bay.

Thoughts of "fireworks" filled his mind as he nosed Black Beauty, the five-five, onto the highway at dawn's sparkling glow. He inhaled deeply, completely filling his lungs, like a carburetor sucking air at peak RPM. His mental capacity flooded with patriotic thoughts as his minds eye superimposed last night's fireworks on the clear Kansas sky.

OH BEAUTIFUL FOR SPACIOUS SKIES. This canopy, so immense, it expands as high as the heavens and as broad as needed, not unlike a blanket of freedom, to cover Americans wherever they might be. The courageous blue makes up the bed for the stars of our flag and the blood red sunsets remind us, daily, of lives surrendered to protect the men, women and children of this vast beauty.

Winding second gear to 80 he dusted off a string of six cars, slammed into third and didn't back off until the needle crested 100. It felt good being an American, serving his country and protecting the ones he loved. The farm-fresh scented air of America's cereal bowl, forced through fully cranked opened cozy wings, fortified his euphoric pride.

FOR AMBER WAVES OF GRAIN. Gold nuggets of life sustaining sustenance on whose shoulders all of those who seek the protection of the spacious skies depend.

The twin quads, allowing the little two-sixty-five - V8 to loaf along at 80+ in the speed-limitless flats of eastern Colorado, got him to within sight of the magnificent Rockies well before sunset. Buck was again stirred to his deep love of God and country.

FOR PURPLE MOUNTAIN MAJESTIES: Forging straight up from the great plains of gilded grain, like a church spire paying homage to the heavens, these rugged resplendent pinnacles symbolize the strength and tenacity of the spacious sky people.

Turning South to catch U.S. 66 he marveled at the abundance of good will in each town he passed as other drivers and pedestrians alike waved or tipped a cap to him.

ABOVE THE FRUITED PLAIN: Scattered among the violet mountains and meadows of wheat are the bounteous production yards of the fruits of American ingenuity and manufacturing. In the history of the world these plains and majestic plateaus have yielded the highest standards of excellence and an excellent people.

Spending tens of hours alone on America's highways after a night of pitching woo and witnessing aerial displays of "bombs bursting in air" can sober even the most dedicated of hot rodders. Somewhere between Santa Fe and Flagstaff, Buck realized that some dreams were meant to be just that and if he was going to sow any wild oats he'd better do it in a hurry. If the Navy keeps its promise he'll be 21 when he's released and old enough to stop playing and start earning his way in this wonderful country.

Last night Katy had told him that she couldn't, or did she say wouldn't, wait forever. One thing sure, the Town Coach could wait, forever if necessary. He'd had his fun with cars. All through high school he had belonged to a car club and had helped build some of the fastest rods between the Rockies and the Mississippi.

Say, maybe he could use some of his machinist skills he was learning, courtesy of his Uncle Sam, and his automobile savvy to start a little business of his own. Yeah, that's it, a custom rod shop. No wait, a new car dealership that sponsored race cars. The possibilities were endless - only in America.

AMERICA - AMERICA: Saying it once isn't enough. To be an American is to be strong and fair, and honest and wise, and humanistic and realistic, and all the other virtuous attributes of those under the protection of the spacious skies.

He could see it all quite clearly now. Katy waiting behind a picket fence, two or three future rodders tugging at her apron strings, as he arrived home nightly in the latest model car from his prosperous agency. They would sit in rocking chairs on the porch every night after dinner and nod hellos to passing neighbors. Each Sunday they'd walk their children to the church where the minister would always point out some good deed he or Katy had done for the little town.

GOD SHED HIS GRACE ON THEE: The Lord truly has blessed us with his benevolence, a covenant with all Americans, to do right by thee and thou and you and me.

Behind the cottage they called home would be his personal experimental garage where some of the hottest rods in the world would be built. He would open the shop to high school kids so they too could learn hot rodding.

AND CROWN THY GOOD WITH BROTHERHOOD: As we keep the compact with God so shall he continue to bestow the munificence that comes from loving and understanding, and helping our brothers and sisters.

Thump, thump, wump...flap, flap.... The reality of a flat tire brought Buck down from his supercharged castles in the clouds. It was almost 0600 Saturday. His daydreaming had caused him to slow his pace and now he was at least three hours from the station.

With the flat tire riding shotgun, because he didn't want to take the time to repack the trunk, he brought the nosed and decked, two door hardtop to peak RPM in first and second as he struggled to set his mind to the business at hand.

Arriving with only a piston stroke or two to spare he vowed to write Katy that night and tell of his dreams and how much of a part he hoped she'd play in them. The view of the fleet, back-dropped by the morning glow of the Pacific, further cemented Buck's faith in himself, his country and the future.

FROM SEA TO SHINING SEA: Not just from Maine to Hawaii or Alaska to Florida, but to wherever those whose roots stem from the fruited plains, the fields of grain or the majestic mountains. For it is the duty of all Americans, an obligation that evolves from a pact with God, to stay the course and expand the spacious skies of brotherhood and freedom.

THE VETTE

As it got closer his suspicions were confirmed — it was a vintage Corvette. Too bad he wasn't driving his old Vette. It could be a fun run over these delightfully twisty and hilly country roads in the outback of the great state of Indiana. Within minutes, on a long straight stretch, the red, with white inset, fifty-nine/sixty two-seater made its bid to pass.

The familiar rumble of the twin pipes indicated the engine was of the solid lifter variety which only made the longing, the recollections, even stronger. What surprised him was that the driver was a lady, a smart looking young lady with long, flame-red hair that trailed out over the rear deck of her open roadster.

Memories of another redhead in a Corvette, back when the Vette was new, quickened his pulse and flooded his mind. She gave a quick look and a smile at mid point, just as she smacked third gear and dumped a set of quads. And with a chirp of rubber she was gone.

A glance at his speedometer told him that the little excitement had caused him to push his seventy-two El Camino to well above the legal limit. Ah, there was a time when he would have relished a high speed run, but at fifty-three years of age and driving a "stocker," Jack Cambry knew better.

Twenty miles on down the road he still couldn't shake the memory of Natalie. It came back in a rush overwhelming his mind — everything from her in-bred sophistication, to the time in the back seat of her fifty- five Bel-Air; strains of "their song," the Crew Cuts, *Angels in the Sky*, playing softly over the radio. He hadn't thought of her in a long time and was confused as to why her familiarity — the longing — was so strong. Perhaps it was the guilt that ground the spider gears of his mind.

She had a long pony tail the first time they met. He had just transferred to a new school and she had come over to him during that first recess. He was lonely and scared but she flipped her pony tail and just said, "Hi, I'm Natalie and I hope you like it here," or something to that effect. Her hair was a soothing deep auburn not the fire red of a Rita Hayworth. They were standing under the pavilion watching the sixth graders in a game of kickball.

She was nice and very pretty but he never let on that he thought so...must have been afraid of getting teased or just too young or something. Funny how some recollections are crystal clear and others are hazy.

Their first date hadn't been for four more years until they were sixteen and he had wheels. Now that he thought about it she was his first real date. Oh, he'd met girls at the Saturday matinee and even kissed a few at games of post office or spin the bottle. But Natalie was the first real date. He couldn't remember how they came to go out, maybe it was when a gang of kids were all standing around the soda fountain at Richter's Pharmacy talking about the up-coming sock hop. Yeah, that was it. She said to nobody in particular, but she was looking at him, that she wanted to go but didn't have a ride.

He laughed to himself remembering that first date. Why she ever went out with him again after he made a total fool of himself was a mystery. He had tried to ace some cat in a '52 Olds away from a light but stalled by dumping the clutch on an under revved engine. Not very cool on a first date. But, the car was cool, as only a Corvette could be.

She was some dish. Not only was she tom-boyish good-looking, but she had a `55 Chev. She had removed the hood and trunk ornaments in preparation for a nose and deck job on this Power-pack stick and had installed spinner hubcaps and a chrome air cleaner herself. She knew more about cars than most guys. She was perfect. Even at sixteen and until they parted at eighteen they fit together, like a valve to a keeper or a connecting rod to a wrist pin.

They had such fun together, he, Natalie and the Vette. They almost never missed a Sunday at the drag strip. He'd be stuck in "B" Sports Car against a lot of usually faster machines and she'd run his Corvette in the Powder Puff class and pull trophy most every time.

How'd it happen? They'd dated — gone steady actually — broken up, then got back together just before his car club's annual dance. Yeah, that was it, the evening of the Knights' big dance when he got pulled by Herb's '57 Fury that everyone had said was a dog. It was no stocker. To this day he was sure Herb had a Isky Five-Cycle cam and maybe more cubes than came from the factory.

He was angry all evening and when they all stopped at Spooner's drive-in for an after dance Coke he had tried to put the make on Herb's date. That was also the night Natalie had picked to tell him her Dad had been transferred out of state. He had only meant to get back at Herb for goading him into a race that was a set-up in the first place.

Though they saw each other a few more times before he left for college and she for Chicago, he never really got a chance to apologize or anything. The next year was a little hazy. He had gotten involved with some chick at OSU, rushed a fraternity and flunked out of school. Next thing he knew he was in the Navy.

Wow, the parade of memories from just seeing an old car — an old Corvette — driven by a red headed honey! Oh, he'd thought about her, especially when the loneliness of military life had almost consumed him and again when he committed himself to marriage.

He believed he had really been in love with Sue Ellen, but, Natalie was always somewhere deep in the reserve fuel tank of his mind. When Sue Ellen left him [maybe he never was really and completely committed to her] he had hunted for Natalie. The search only lasted until he learned she was married.

****

The yellow diamond shaped sign indicated a right followed by a left, both with a suggested safe speed of forty. He knew he wasn't in a Corvette and he wasn't in his twenties, but the urge was too great as he set the classic pick-up into the first bend at a little over 70. He rode it through on rails pretending it was a four wheel drift, getting hard on the gas at the apex of each turn. It felt good, speed, engine noise...memories.

Daydreaming sure does help while the miles away. Already he was over halfway to Chicago. It had been such a beautiful day that he had driven the old way through the countryside of farm belt America, the route before the Interstate.

Slowing for a small burg he noticed the red and white Vette parked at the side of a Shell station. Well, he needed gas anyway, and Shell was one of the cards he carried. It sure wouldn't hurt to take a few minutes to look at the vehicle of the past hour's recollections.

A cursory exam of the sports car yielded the knowledge that it was a 1959 model and had a 6500 RPM red line on the tach which indicated it came with a factory 270 or 290 horsepower engine. Absorbed in a world of automobilia he didn't see her until she was standing right next to him.   "Excuse me, sir. I'd like to get into my car."

She couldn't have been much more than twenty-five and could have passed as Natalie's twin if it were thirty plus years ago.

"I'm sorry. I was just admiring your Vette. Had it long?"

"Well, we've owned it for about five years but it was only in the last six months that we've had the time and money to get it into running shape," she said with a smile that showed a slight over bite.

"You are a credit to Corvette owners of old by the way you handled it back there on the open road. Drove like a pro or your daddy owns the road," he joked, trying to expand the moment.

"Wrong on both counts, mister. I'm not a professional and my daddy died last year. So if you'll excuse me...."

"I'm sorry for intruding. It's just that this car stirred thoughts of another Corvette and another red head too many years ago. The car got traded and the red head...I guess she's lost forever."

She reached for the door handle, stopped, turned toward him and said, "No, I'm the one who should be sorry. I'm not in a good mood. I just broke up with my boy friend. I know you old timers get all twisted out of shape at the sight of machines like this. Uh, the car has the original two-eighty-three engine, bored sixty thousandths over, twin four barrels and an oh-two-seven, solid-lifter, Duntov cam powered through a four- speed transmission and four-eleven, Posi-traction rear axle.

"Say, you do know your stuff. Learn it from your dad? He asked, trying not to sound conciliatory.

"I learned mostly from my mom. It's her car and we made a project of rebuilding it. We had the mechanical work done at a shop in Cincinnati, that's where my mom's from. We did the interior and all the body work ourselves, except the final paint," the red-haired beauty stated proudly.

At the mention of Cincinnati and a widow who knew cars, a chill with the speed of a small-block Chevy, swept over him. An intense smile exposed a face full of age lines as his clear hazel eyes studied her features — red hair, the slightly up-turned nose, the high cheek bones and that slight overbite with very small teeth....

"Why are you looking at me like that? Are you going to hit on me, pal? Come on, let me get into my car I've got places to go," she scolded, brushing past him to vault into the drivers seat.

"I'm, I'm sorry," he stammered. "Was...is you mother's name, Wilson?"

"No, Her name's Minderman. Now please let me go." She twisted the key firing up all eight cylinders with the unmistakably familiar throaty roar of the short-stroke Chevy.

With a rap of the accelerator that sent the little engine revving past three grand she lifted the "T" handle and slapped the lever into reverse. He stepped back, smarting from the false and brash accusation, still overwhelmed by the memories and similarities. He looked at his shoes waiting for her to back away.

The Vette, engine loping at seven-hundred-fifty RPM, didn't move. He snuck a glance. Maybe he was still in her way. Boy was he embarrassed. The girl with Rita Hayworth hair and the features of a teenage lost love was staring at him, mouth agape.

Barely audible, over the rumble of the two-seventy, he heard her say, "Yes. You mean my mother's *maiden* name? Yeah, it was Wilson. Did you know her?" She turned her head as if checking the rear view mirror then turned back again, eyes wide. "Oh wow! If your name's Jack then my mom's been looking for you."

THE ANNOUNCER

Atop the control tower
at any drag race
runs the announcer's mouth
at a constant and fever pace.

"Hey, is this thing on? Hello... Hello.... Allllright we got the power. How 'bout it race fans. Are all you cats and chicks having a good time? Sure 'nuff, this the Ol' Isky comin' at ya from atop the control tower. Crazy man.

"Welcome to the Beechmont Dragway a project of SOTA, the Southern Ohio Timing Association, and all the affiliated clubs in the area. This is a National Hot Rod Association sanctioned strip, sure 'nuff, and we will be going by their rules. Do ya dig, man.

"N.H.R.A. strips mean only one person will be

allowed in any car during any run - qualifying, grudge or elimination. All open bodied cars must have safety belts and roll bars. No snap on hub caps on any cars. With the exception of stock and gas classes all cars must be equipped with flywheel shields. Open or altered class drivers must wear a safety approved helmet and goggles. If you have any questions see the Strip Marshal in the staging area.

"First off we have a few announcements. The ice man hasn't made the scene yet so if you're in need of a cold Coke or somethin' you're gonna have to wait. He is expected within the hour. Next all you cats who plan on racing today please use gate "B" as in baby, baby, baby. And, for you squirrels and shot-rodders, no pealing out on the return strip. No trophies will be awarded in classes with fewer than two cars and for the first time trophies will be awarded for the new classifications of "A" through "E" Stock AUTOMATIC. Powder Puffs will be run after top eliminator.

"Attention all you good lookin' chicks. We're going to have a short-shorts contest a little later on. Don't sweat it, just mosey on down to the control tower so as ol' Isky can rest his eyes on fine lookin' chicks, sure 'nuff. The winner of the contest will get to hand out the trophies to the winners in each class. Oh yeah, the Times-Star is expected to be here for the top eliminator run and trophy presentation. So ya might get your picture in the newspaper. Crazy man.

"Well, lookie here. There's a cat with a chick on each arm. There must be some dragstrip rule against that. Sure 'nuff, I'll look it up. My the red head is...yeah I'm talking about you - Hi baby come up and see ol' Isky if he doesn't pay enough attention to ya, ya dig?

"From now until two o'clock we will have tune-up runs and grudge matches. If you want to run a grudge match please be sure and let the flagman know before approaching the line.

"I've just been informed that Bob 'Cookie' Cook and his Red Monster has arrived at the inspection station. This is going to be a swell day. The Red Monster, in case some of you clods don't know, is a jet engine powered "A" Dragster that was one of the first machines to break one-fifty-five for the standing quarter mile. Rumor has it he's set to try one-six-oh today!

"Well, look what just burned rubber all the way to the starting line: Tiny's "B" Altered Coupe. Sounds good, but then all Chevy's sound good to a GMC man. Whoa...he almost let it get away from him. Better try feathering the gas if you can't get slicks on that thing. We don't have a back-up flagman today so try to take it easy, okay guys! Besides, Marty is a little hung over and really isn't in the mood to make an ambulance run, sure 'nuff. Tiny's run was one-oh-two point six.

"Big Bart's "D" Gas '49 Ford is coming into the staging area now. Ol' Isky was there when BB christened her on Reading Road a few days ago. That flathead's sporting eight-deuces, and a poked and stroked Merc engine, sure 'nuff. Ah...the sound of a flathead is still sweet music even to this die hard Chevy man. Uh, oh. Looks like somethin' broke. I don't see any smoke so it must be in the drive train. Put back in the mud, or put a Chevy in it, sure 'nuff.

"I don't know how many of you cats can see over to the south end of the pit area, but there's this chick that's been just chewin' some cat out, for what seems like the longest time. He better listen up real good 'cuz she's one good lookin' little lady. Got a long pony tail that just keeps bouncin' up and down as she shakes her finger at him. I don't know what she's sayin' or what he did. He's just standin' there with his head hung down, a wrench in one hand and leaning up against a "B" Altered Coupe. Man, she's really giving it to him, sure 'nuff.

"All right it's time for the contest. All you chicks in short-short attire come on down to just under the control tower. Oh, I see we've already got a bevy of beauties here now, sure 'nuff. My, oh my, we do have some lovelies here today. Now, if I was the judge, I'd pick the first one who climbs up into this tower with me, sure 'nuff.

"Sorry for the distraction. While my attention was on more pleasant things the "B" Altered Coupe of the cat from Middletown, the one who was getting chewed out by that cute little blond, turned a one-oh-nine, three. That will make quite an interesting race against Tiny's rod in the trophy run. It appears that they are the only two in that class today. Now, wait a minute. I don't know what's goin' on but the chick

who was ballin' out the Middletown cat in the pits a little while ago is now holding hands with Tiny! This has all the makings of the race of the day. Altered Coupe against Altered Coupe and maybe the winner gets the girl, sure 'nuff.

"Allllright! They have selected the trophy girl and is she a honey. Ol' Isky's gonna have a personal interview with her a little later. I'll tell ya all about it...tomorrow.

"If you cats and chicks will turn your attention to the staging area there's one cherry "B" Street Roadster revvin' up. Man, he must have a thousand hand rubbed coats of candy apple red lacquer on that machine. We'll know in a minute if it runs as good as it looks. Sounds good, here's the flag. He got off the line okay. It appears to have three-two's on an overhead valve something - got a little rubber in second gear - hold your horses, times coming in up...see ya later alligator, ninety-six point three! Not bad. Bet it'll run the pants off anything Harry High-school can borrow from his daddy, sure 'nuff.

"They have just informed me that the elimination runs begin in thirty minutes. The ice man has arrived - cold Cokes and Pepsi's now available at the concession stand. So, ol' Isky, sure 'nuff, is gonna take a break. Gonna make like a tree and leaf, put an egg in my shoe and beat it, if ya dig what I mean. Crazy man.

****

"Ol' Isky's back and ready for the final elimination runs of the day. Looks like same old same fifty-seven Chev verses fifty-seven Chev for Super Stock. We've got two fuelies. The near lane, a two-door One- Fifty and the other a convertible that's had a nose and deck job. Man, they sure can burn those tires. Looks like the convertible got half a car on the start but here comes the two-door. Ninety-two point seven to the far lane, crazy man.

"The trophies will be presented by the winner of our short-shorts contest, Miss Shirley Cravens of Hartwell. Shirley's a Junior at Woodward High. She's also jail bait fellahs, so don't even think about it, sure 'nuff!

"We're now set for the Altered Coupe trophy run and I don't know about you cats, but I want to know who gets the chick with the pony tail. I wonder if one cat knows that the other cat is trying to cut his time or who the chick came with in the first place. Crazy man.

"Hold everything. Paul, Marty, fellow Knights, any available members of the day crew. Please head for the staging area. The two Altered Coupe drivers know of each other, sure 'nuff, sure 'nuff. They're out of their cars and, for the moment, just shouting back and forth. We don't want any fisticuffs here so if you guys can hear me; knock it off, ya dig.

"You guys in the staging area just hold your horses 'till things get settled down. This isn't 'Rebel Without A Cause' - we don't want any rumbles.

"Alright the Strip Marshal is there and all is okay. This run is going to be one hot race. I'd give next week's pay to know who Pony Tail is rooting for.

"Tiny's machine is a '41 Willy's that's been chopped and sectioned. The red primer leaves a lot to be desired - beauty wise. But, knowing Tiny, the paint job, if he ever gets around to it, will be as good as his engine work. The mill is a two-eighty-three Chevy with Lathum Supercharger, Iskenderian five-cycle cam and Mallory ignition.

"This info just in on the hep cat from Middletown. He's piloting a three-window '32 Ford that's been chopped, channeled and finished with a beautiful orange and red flame job over royal blue lacquer. Twin four barrel carbs power his naturally aspired fifty-six Caddy engine. Word is he did all the work, including the paint, except the flame job, himself. The transmission....

'They're at the starting line. Look at the flames shooting from the collector pipes on the near lane

Chevy powered Willy's. The noise from that little Chevy is sure 'nuff deafening. Pony tail is motionless on the sideline, hands pressing against her ears like everyone else.

"It's a fair start! The Caddy powered rod shoots to a early lead - the far lane coupe over spins, billows of smoke coming from his tires as he fights for traction - mid-point the blown two-eighty-three rockets ahead but the torque of the big caddy pulls him even - at the line it's, it's...the near lane at one, one, two, six a new track record for "B" Altered Coupe. Sure 'nuff, folks.

"Hang tight now. Top Eliminator contenders, the Red Monster and a Chrysler powered "A" Dragster, are lining up in the staging area now.

"Hey you guys, clear the return lane for the two altered coupes. How 'bout a big hand for them. That was some race, record and all. Maybe Shirley will give each of them a kiss along with the trophy - if pony tail doesn't mind, sure 'nuff. Say what happened to her? The two coupe drivers are standing side by side and she's no where to be found.

"If you can hear me over the dragster's roar, the far lane holds Bob Cook's Allis Chalmers powered set of rails. He's going for the track record of one-fifty-nine while trying to stave off the challenge for Top Eliminator from Billy Anders' blown and injected Chrysler Hemi... they're off - Anders has the lead but here comes the jet powered Red Monster - it's the near lane, but, the Red Monster has cracked the one-sixty limit. Anders beat the Monster to the finish line but Cookie has a new track record of one-sixty-one point eight. Crazy man.

"While we wait for the trophy winner and the track record holder to come by the control tower for their awards I have a few final announcements to make. The Southern Ohio Timing Association wishes to thank...."

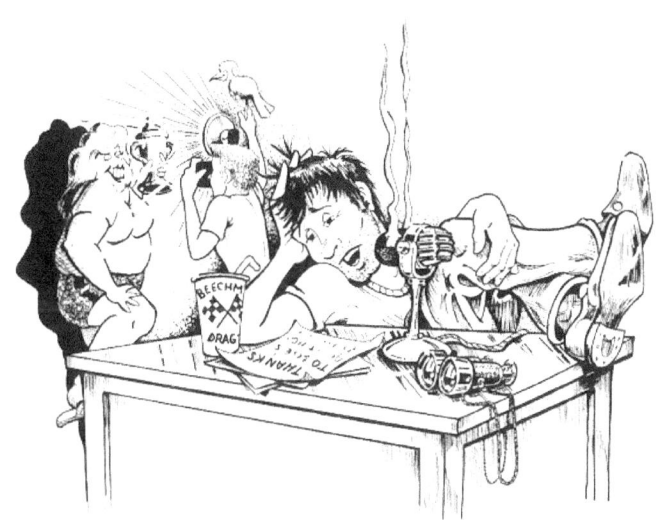

SECOND LOVE

Corvettes, BMWs, cars with only numbers for identification, a few Porsches and Cadillacs plus a gaggle of yesterday's lot-fatigued sports- cars-du-jour crowded around my '48 Town & Country. That should have been the first clue that I didn't fit in. I mean any dumbie can drive the latest mega-gadget phallic-mobile. Well, any dumbie with boxes of Ben Franklins to toss around.

The event was the monthly singles' party at the Art Museum — how's that for sophistication. Recently singled I thought I'd try this nineties method of counterpart-matching. The tendered palatable amenities were of a higher value than the six bucks admission price, and the cast of hundreds of single men and women was as energized and coercive as the rock & roll band.

Mingling among the sea of Day-Glo orange name tags a very pretty and articulate lass with tresses of blonde curls and clear brown eyes asked me to hold her purse while she did something with her hair. The generic conversation went something like: "Sure is crowded...what-ja- say...music's great...what...?" However, I learned too late the problem with these cosmopolitan gatherings. It seems that while trying to concentrate on the night's best cull I couldn't help noticing the pick of the week followed by surely a centerfold of the month as they faded in and out of my view. My failure of not being able to focus on this fine specimen of Americana might have been one of the reasons she left — on the pretext of having to visit the lady's room. No problem she'll be back. Not.

Smiling my way around the enormous hall I was quietly hailed by an old friend. Even way back in high school my long lost buddy was known as a real catch. So, I figured if I just hung around the creme de la creme would rise to the occasion. Good thinking, slick!

No sooner had our hands clasped in the obligatory handshake than a lovely lady, naturally known to my friend, thrust her perfect 36C's into our midst. I lost all track of time, food, drink and even the brown eyed blond not to mention the pick of the week/centerfold. Boy was she something — but words, even to this seasoned Hemingway fan, cannot be found to describe a dream of a lady that was so, so.... So long. Turns out she's into S&M.

I don't think these high pressure, one-upmanship mass gatherings are for me. Maybe I'll try the city's magazine for a more subtle approach.

DWPM/NS, novelist, 5'9", 160. Attractive, trim, ethically/morally sound, romantic, well mannered, old school gentleman. Hoping to discover latent brilliant cut counterpart among pseudo gems to satiate desire for commitment. Letter w/photo please.

Yeah, well it was worth a shot and I know, I know, I lied about being a novelist, but I'm working on one. For a few bucks, and total anonymity, I might meet the lady with whom I will blissfully spend the rest of my life. Finding a true and staple mate (or is it stable mate?) — that's the hard part.

Outta sight. Eight letters! Exhilaration short lived. Two were form letters, three could hardly write, two others that seemed to be very materialistic — then there was....

Dear Novelist,

I loved your ad and if you are what you say you are you just might have discovered a true Ideal-D-Flawless. I am degreed DWPF/NS, 5'5", 135 Gray/Blond & Blue. Additionally, I am filthy rich and count among my closest personal friends, Laura Bush, Alanis Morisette, and Curt Cobain (well, at least until he had the audacity to kill himself). Life, of course, will not be perfect until I find an impeccably mannered and romantic, real gentleman with whom to share the rest of my life. But, enough about you.

I am a commercial artist but yearn to be a free-lance portraitist. I am a product of the local school system having been born and raised in the east suburbs. Today, I live in a cramped loft, but with northern light. Though I tend to lean to the right, I am very straight. My nature and demeanor is flexible, except when it comes to morals and ethics. Hobbies include, reading, the city's cultural accommodations and an occasional round of tennis.

My ideal companion will have all of the attributes you list in your ad plus, he, like me, yearns for someone to be back-to-back, shoulder-to-shoulder, belly-to-belly....

Shall we begin to build ways
To learn about you and me
Interrelating at events
To see what we shall see?

If you find me interesting please write with pic to my P.O. Box. Oh yeah, I made up the part about being filthy rich and the personal friend list. Hey, if you can't take a joke....

Judy

Sometimes ya get lucky. Better not screw this up, slick. Clear the calendar it's time to ink the stationery.

Dear Judy,

Enjoyed your letter on this sunny day
You seem like the kind of girl
I would like to get to know
And hopefully make your toes curl

Anyway, and aside from being a great guy, I am also a staunch proponent of intercourse — wait, wait I left a word out: SOCIAL — it goes before intercourse as in I like talking and listening to a lady who is mentally active. This is just awful! We haven't even met and already you probably think I'm some kind of sex machine. I'm so embarrassed.

On the plus side: I never lie, cheat or steal. Well, that's not exactly all true; I might steal your heart, if....

So if you're still reading maybe there's a chance. Just now I was daydreaming of your visit to my historic downtown row house for a little fireside tête-à-tête. Nothing is more soothing in the Fall of the year than viewing ancient classic roof tops through floor-to-ceiling, paned-windows from which the likes of the Chimney Sweep, the Fiddler and Mary Poppins can surely be glimpsed. A slight chill in the air while we listen to manmade music as the natural sounds of crackling fire and city...are we in love yet — I'm getting carried away — (see I told you I was a romantic).

Alright, already we're now coming to final options. You're either going to:

a) Foolishly crumple this up and throw it away;

b) Grab the phone and call;

c) Send me a big giant box stuffed full of gifts & toys & things;

d) Drive to 1621 Main and beat on my door;

e) Call your lawyer.

David

She called, she called, she called! Wow. It's done — sealed. Kaldi's Coffee House tomorrow at seven.

I got there early, maybe five minutes. Three minutes later a silvery-haired ribbon of silk and boots drifted through the jostling crowd. "I sure hope you're Judy," I hushed to a face of character and eyes of maturity as she floated toward me.

"Only if you're David," she smiled.

"Kiss my finger," I grinned, impetuously holding up my index finger.

Her smile broadened as her lips lightly brushed the calluses before she asked, "Why?"

"Dear Diary, the first thing she did was kiss me," I impishly replied.

Between sips of licorice flavored herbal tea and in a lifetime measured in short hot flashes, we melded souls in wispy and sometimes intellectual conversation. I'm not sure if the quaint bistro was crowded or if the three-piece jazz combo was in good form as I only saw two cyan eyes and heard the concussion of bells superimposed on my mind. The lady named Judy stirred feelings of emotional splendor never before experienced.

Perhaps it was the tea, or just destiny that caused strong and compelling interaction from the very first encounter. We fit together like a soft playing radio to a padded dash. Before the night ended, it seemed, Burns and Allen style, we were finishing each others sentences — sometimes without even talking.

In a tiny booth designed for esoteric confidences we talked, laughed, bantered and oozed vibes far later than we both were accustomed to being out. Somewhere between the late night and early morning hours I told her, "This is fun and I really like being with you. The similarities are startling. The way you talk, look, laugh, well, ah," I stammered, examining my hands. "You really remind me of; let me count...my second wife. Yeah, that's it, wife number two."

I knew her mouth dropped open in indignation, but her voice was smiling. "Your second wife! How, how, many wives have you had?"

Keeping my eyes downcast, I took a sip of tea after which I slowly dabbed the napkin at the corners of my mouth. Then, still suppressing a grin, I touched the back of her hand with one finger, looked up, and matched her smile as I whispered, "Only one."

SUMMER OF '57

Three deuces on an open roadster
Puppy love with a pony tail
Eye tearing wind at a hundred per
The summer of '57 - all hail

Seven-thirty Sunday morning, Wynnie, so named because he always wore the black and red T-shirts that advertised the oil additive, Wynn's Friction Proofing, picked me up for the strip. He was going to be the announcer for the day while I was to fill in wherever they needed slave labor. BB, Big Bart, didn't have to work the strip today, but promised to be down later now that his full race '49 primered Ford had a new axle. Wynnie's '32 still wasn't ready to race, so we motored down through the quiet residential neighborhoods in his Stude-a-lac, the deep twin Glas-pacs shattering the morning stillness as he backed off for hills and stop lights. The "Stude" part was a 1953 Studebaker with orange and yellow flames licking 12 coats of coal black lacquer. The "lac" was, of course, a late model Cadillac engine. Being among the first to arrive, we stopped at the check-in to register and paint "C" GAS and the number one on his rear side window before heading to the pit area.

As soon as we got air cleaners from atop the twin four-barrel carbs and the hub caps removed, Wynnie, wearing his trademark T-shirt, took off for the announcer's stand. Out in front of this two story observation post I grabbed a broom to sweep the burned rubber and other debris off the strip. I was thankful for the job, since it didn't require much thought. My mind was still in a daze from last night and I couldn't stop thinking about Kathy.

The strip does have magic. Nothing can dampen the exuberance of a hot rodder nestled among dreams on wheels. The taste of oil tainted dust, the unmistakable smells of gasoline, alcohol and other exotic fuels had a calming, yet exciting, grip on us all.

Early arrivals were greeted by songs of Bobwhite Quail, crickets and other natural morning sounds. In an hour rodders and spectators alike would ride the crest of waves of eardrum numbing roars from the fire shooting machines whose exhaust looked like giant acetylene torches as they battled to be the fastest.

As the pit began to fill with hot-rods and stockers, I was surprised to see Joey in a '57 Chev with "B/S 22" on the window. Joey was a year ahead of me in school and one of those stuck up Harry-high-school types. He was a little taller and heavier than I, but he'd probably run from a fight.

Taking a short break during the practice runs I sauntered over to his car. I didn't really like him but he was dating Kathy's friend, Donna, and maybe I could pump him for a little info on Kathy.

"Where'd you get the wheels, man?" I asked, turning my shoulder toward him so he couldn't help but notice my official Lakewood Timing Association armband. He might have a drivers license, but I was a member of THE club, as in builders and operators of the drag strip.

"I borrowed my dad's car, It's stock but at least it's a stick," he said, as he struggled to pull the air cleaner off the power-packed V8 engine.

"Does he know that you're going to race it?"

"Heck no, I told him I was going on a school picnic."

"Ah man, school ain't started yet."

"I'm hep, but I told him it was a pre-school meeting of the drama club, ya dig."

"You don't think he'll be a little suspicious when you come rollin' in with numbers painted on the window, no hub caps and covered with dust?" I asked incredulously.

"Not a chance. I'll take it to a car wash first.

"So Joey, where's your chick, Donna?"

"Donna's going to meet me later. By the way she told me Kathy was going to Coney today with some other cat and I just figured that since she's not with you now...you didn't make-out so good. That Kathy's some looker, I wouldn't mind a piece of that so..., ah, how'd you, ah, make-out last night," he sneered, like Kathy was dirty or some kind of trashy girl.

I didn't even have to think, I just started my right toward his jaw. It was only a glancing blow but my following left connected hard with his mouth. He got in a return light jab to my forehead before we locked in a wrestling match our arms and legs entwined, like spaghetti in a bowl as we writhed and twisted on the ground. Joey was just trying to protect himself, but I was hot and mad. It took both of the cats working on the "A" altered coupe adjacent to us to pull me off. Joey was covered with dirt and had a split lip. But, I was just a little dusty.

I walked away throwing over my shoulder, "Watch your mouth, punk or next time there won't be anyone to pull me off." I felt really cool and tough, and my legs were shaking. I thought about calling Joey's old man to tell him where he could find the family bus.

Back to the staging area, I picked up my broom and swept up a storm while thoughts of Kathy with another guy banged around inside my head. Maybe she was just going with her brother and mother and Joey was just jesting me. Yeah, sure. Maybe she had a date with some big bruiser and they were rolling around on the sand right now. I had to find a phone. The thought of her in a bathing suit was, like crazy, and the thought of her in a bathing suit with another guy was...I didn't want to think about it. If he was a big beast, maybe I could get some of my fellow club members to kick his tail. The sound of a revved engine brought me back to reality. I didn't feel so good.

I don't remember too much of the rest of the day other than Wynnie won the "C" Gas trophy and BB blew his pressure plate, again on his maiden run. It didn't look like he was ever going to get to the end of the strip. The only highlight of the whole day, if you can call it that, was when the clutch blew in some kid's brand new '57 Chevy. It didn't just break or quit - it exploded. I mean parts of the disk and plate came through the floor board, through the dash board and through the windshield. That nice new car was all tore up. Everybody forgot their own troubles for awhile after that.

****

Slunk down in the shotgun seat of the trophy winning "C-Gasser" Wynnie, noticing I was a little quiet, inquired, "You haven't said much today. Is anything wrong?"

"Naw, I'm just hot, tired and in need of a bath...and I had a date with this chick last night and...."

"Oh, you've got it bad. What did she do to you?"

"Man, I don't know. We had a date last night, went to the passion pit with BB and Janice, and then some guy at the strip said something and...."

"Hey, man, slow down. You're not making any sense. Did she dump you? What about this guy at the strip?"

"I don't know, man, I just don't know anything."

"Man, you ought...."

"Shhhh," I cut Wynnie off as I reached for the volume knob on the radio, turning it up to hear the Fat Man beg for insatiable love with his moaning, wailing ballad, "I'm in love again".

Ever since we heard it together when we first met I felt it had become our song. Maybe she felt the same? Fat chance.

"I'm sorry, what were you saying?" I asked.

"Man, you really got it bad. But I will try to enlighten you with Wynnie's words to live by: When it comes to women just try to remember Wynnie's rule: Kiss 'em all you want, but never put more money in a honey than bread in your sled, if you catch my drift," Wynnie related in a fatherly tone.

Wynnie, a full five years older than me, had sorta taken me under his wing. He was a little over six feet, a little under 200 pounds, and an all day smile. He was also the club secretary and very knowledgeable about cars thus making me one lucky cat.

"Yeah, I know you've told me before that if you take care of a rod it won't let you down whereas girls, no matter how well you treat them, sometimes can't even be jump started," I intoned as memories of last night's fireworks electrified my mind like spark plugs wired to an over- revved magneto. Recollections of her open mouth against mine, her small firm breasts crushing my chest, hands and arms encircling, caressing...I'd trade my rod and any future car for a lifetime of kisses from her, I'd....

We didn't talk much on the rest of the way home and Wynnie left me with the request to use a small part of my garage to build another Cadillac engine he was planning to drop into his '32 Ford roadster.

I was beat. It was almost 6:00 P.M. and I just had to call Kathy. No answer. I showered and got to the dinner table just in time for a hot meal; some kind of fish with rice. It looked good, but I just didn't seem to be hungry. When I realized that I hadn't eaten all day I forced myself to put away two helpings. It wasn't like me not to be hungry, I wondered what was wrong. After dinner I tried to call again; still no answer. Maybe Wynnie was right. This chick could drive me to drink, if I drank. I decided to lie down and take a nap and then try again. The nap lasted fourteen hours!

First thing the next morning my head started to think about all the stuff I had to do; don't call Kathy - wait for her to call me, work on the car, don't call Kathy, get dressed, don't call..., I might as well call her and get it over with. She answered on the second ring.

"Kathy? Hi, it's me."

"Hi, Paul. I was hoping you'd call. I missed not talking to you yesterday. Did you have a good time at the strip?"

Now what. She just said she missed me. Maybe I was wrong, but I better find out just in case.

"What? I'm sorry I didn't hear what you said," I pleaded.

"I said," Kathy began again, "How was your day at the strip? Did Janice go with Bart?"

"No, I think she had to be with her family so BB came alone. He blew his clutch and didn't get to finish even the first practice run." I summoned up some courage and continued. "Did you have a good time at Coney?"

"How did you know I went to Coney?"

"Hey, get hep. I keep tabs on all the good lookin' chicks."

"You must have talked to my mother or brother. Did you?"

"No," I said, starting to feel very confident.

"Well then, how did you know. And did you miss me?"

"Yeah, I would have liked to have seen you at the strip. If you'd been there, you could have seen Joey get the tar beat out of him."

"Oh, that's who told you. It was Joey wasn't it? And what do you mean he had the tar beat out of him? Did his daddy beat him for racing the car?"

"Naw, I punched him out for smart mouthing me."

"You fought him? Why? What did he do?"

"Yeah. He mentioned that you were going to Coney with some guy, that's all," I said, trying to sound cool. "Who'd you go with," I had to ask.

"Just my brother, my mother and a neighbor boy. You hit Joey just for saying that?"

"Well, there might have been other reasons, such as I don't really like the kid in the first place. Who is this neighbor kid? How old is he?"

"His name's Billy and he's sixteen. He lives two doors up the street, if you must know, and I don't like boys who fight," she said, testily.

"Listen, he said some things about you that, well, weren't very nice and I just had to, uh...defend your honor."

"Oh. OH! Thank you, Paul...I think."

"Now back to the main subject, is he a boy friend, or what?"

A little flustered Kathy confessed, "You mean Billy? He's just a friend. I've known him since, like forever." Then regaining her composure she taunted, "Are you jealous?"

"Not me, we're not going steady or anything are we?"

Almost in a whisper she said, "No."

Silence....It's wonders what a good night's sleep can do to clear one's head, I thought, as I began to enjoy the idea that she was impressed that I had defended her honor plus she just might be worried that I might be worried. My heart still said to keep talking, talk forever, but my now clear brain said to shag ass.

"Kathy, I've got to go now. I'm like starved and if I hurry, maybe I can get Bessie to fix me something to eat."

"Who's Bessie?" If you came over here, I'd fix you something."

"If I had wheels I'd be there."

"Who's Bessie?"

"Just a chick I know," I teased.

"How old is this 'chick' and where does she live?"

"Sounds to me like you're the one who's jealous."

"We're not going steady or anything," she mimicked.

"Hey, I'm like gone, I hear Bessie in the kitchen. Just for your information though, Bessie is our laundress and besides that, she's really old - at least 40!"

"You have somebody to do your wash? Why doesn't your mother do it? Does she work?" Kathy blurted out.

"My mom died ten years ago. I'm an orphan," I teased.

"Oh, golly, I'm sorry. I didn't know about your mom...wait a minute. You told me your mother and father have been married for over 20 years."

"Well, maybe I made up that part about the demise of my mom."

"Why you little stinker. I'm going to wash your mouth out with soap."

"Hey, I've really got to go. I'll call you tonight."

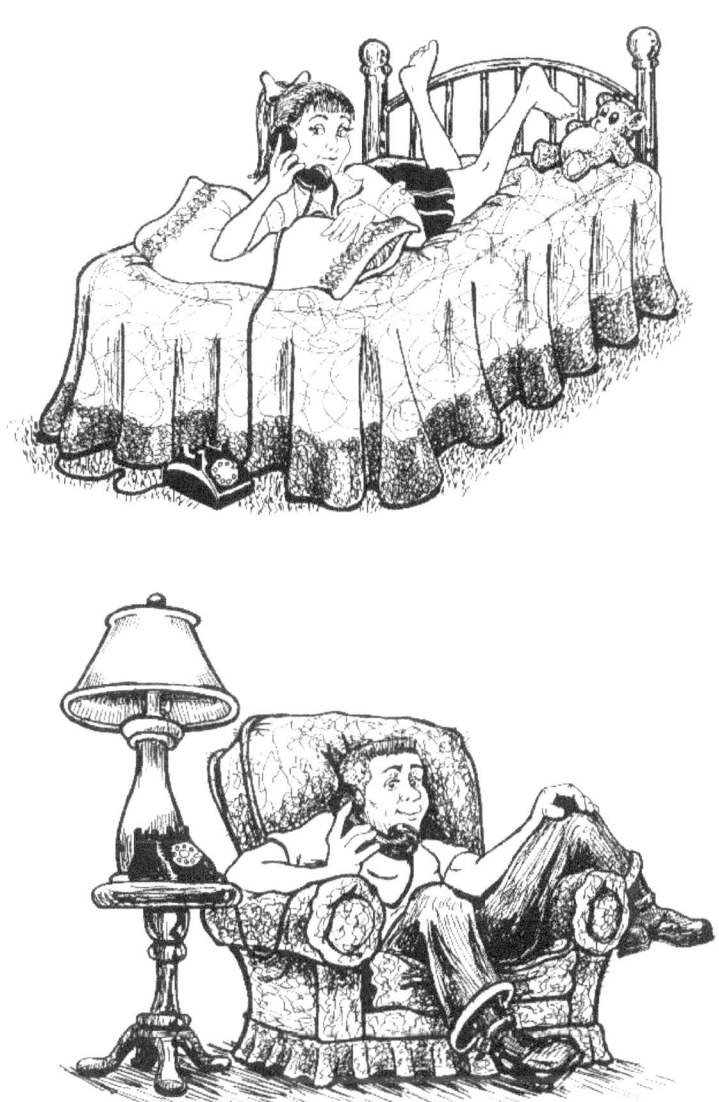

I still didn't know where I stood, but I felt better. I had a lot to digest in addition to food. After a satisfying meal of three eggs fried in bacon grease, and a stack of toast, I went out to the garage and at once decided to finish installing the juice brakes. My rod was a Ford, or rather a conglomeration of a lot of Fords. The frame was a 1932 coupe, the body a Model "T" roadster, and the engine from a '48 truck that my uncle had wrecked.

Wynnie arrived late in the afternoon and we unloaded his Caddy engine block from the trunk of the Stude-a-lac, placing it in the only free corner left in the garage. We didn't talk much, both having work to do. My task seemed insurmountable with the time I had left before I turned sixteen. I needed the rod finished by then so I would have something to drive when I got my license. But, school would start the day after Labor Day, a week from tomorrow. Next Sunday I would have to help my parents get ready for a big party they were giving that night, which meant no drag strip, and Monday, Labor Day, was reserved for cleaning up after the party.

I worked every day that week on the little roadster, and a few nights too. Kathy and I talked on the phone night after night, sometimes for hours on end. She didn't say anything more about the boy next door and I didn't ask, but in the back of my mind I knew that trouble could come from that type of relationship. After all, didn't Mickey Rooney and Judy Garland live next door to each other in the Andy Hardy movies? Come to think of it I had a girl next door. Judy Bloom, a real looker. In fact, just last week she and her mother had been over to bring my mom some community stuff. She even stopped in the garage and watched me work, asking all kinds of questions about the job at hand. I don't think I was very nice to her because at the time I was doing the frustrating operation of setting the valves and had to devote all my attention to that. Maybe she liked me. Hummmm! I don't need more girl problems. However, I just might mention her to Kathy if she ever said anything about the cat who lived next to her. Why does everything have to be so complicated?

Saturday rolled around with a light rain falling - a perfect day to finish the engine. The flathead mill I was hopping up, from my uncle's '48 truck, was now better than new. I had wanted to stuff a Chevy V8 between the rails but even used-Chevy engines were expensive. Besides I had gotten my powerplant from my uncle, for free. Painstakingly I had ported and polished the .030-over block, fitted with 3-ring racing pistons and installed a Potvin Super three-eighth cam. Today, I would fit number 71 power jets and number 41 main jets in the three Stromberg 97's that sat atop the Evans manifold. Time permitting I would also torque the 8½ to 1 Sharp heads and fit the Auto Pulse electric fuel pump to the frame right next to the gas tank.

It was almost seven when I finally decided to call it a day. Mom fixed soup and a sandwich which she made me eat in the garage because the kitchen was filled with stuff for the party and besides, I was too dirty. Still hungry, I conned her for a few quarters for a piece of pie at Carters'. A quick wash up in the garage spigot and a little axle grease to help my crew cut stand up and 1 cut-out to hitch-hike to the drive-in.

Home from Carters', I was exhausted and drained from the days tension, I had to call Kathy and tell her about the progress. She wasn't interested so we talked about school and I had to punish myself by asking how she was going to get to school.

"Billy got a car, so he said he'll drive me every day," Kathy answered without a trace of emotion.

"Is it a car pool, or is it just you and Billy?"

"Well, let's see, It's Billy and me and my brother and maybe Donna. Why, are you worried? We're not going steady or anything."

"Would you go steady with me, if I asked?"

"Are you asking?"

"Yeah I'd like to go steady with you."

"Oh, Paul, I don't know. Are you in love with me?" She asked in a hushed tone.

"I think so. How 'bout you Kathy?"

"I know you're in love with your car. Lets not talk about this on the phone. When can I see you?"

"Maybe tomorrow night. You know that big party my parents are throwing? Well, I think I'll be the official valet. See the driveway isn't big enough to hold all the cars, so I'll take the guests' cars when they arrive and park them on the road next to the house. Then, while the party's going on, I might be able to drive one of them over for a visit," I boasted.

"Paul, I don't want you to do anything illegal. What if you get caught?"

"Don't sweat it. Will you come out if you see a strange car outside and hear a horn?"

"Oh, I don't know, I don't want you to get in trouble."

"I'll take my chances. See ya, and I can't wait for tomorrow night."

The merry-go-round was starting to move again. It must have slowed there for a while when I was having delusions about the cat who lived next to Kathy. I knew she loved me, the rod was coming along alright and everything was going to be a-okay.

****

Sunday morning was dry and the sun even looked like it might make an appearance. I worked all day cutting the grass, trimming hedges and washing down the patio furniture. While cutting the grass between the woods and the road, as there were no sidewalks, Jimmy walked by.

"Hey daddy-o, where you been? I've hardly seen you all summer," I asked once I got the big Whirlwind mower shut down.

"Ah man, my old man's had me working for him since the last day of school. But he told me if I could save a hundred bucks by the start of school, he'd buy me a car. I've got a hundred and twenty now. Where the Sam Hill have you been besides working on your car? How's it coming, anyway?" Jimmy said, in rapid fire.

"That's it, just working' on the car, cutting this stupid grass and going to the strip. What kind wheels is your old man gonna get ya?"

"I think I might get lucky. He's talking about a convertible, a Chevy."

"Do you think he'll go for a two-seventy and a stick?" I asked with obvious enthusiasm.

"Not a chance. It will have to be an automatic because my Mom will need to drive it. It will still be one fine honey wagon if he gets the flop top."

"Where are you going now?" I asked.

"I'm just going to get the mail that everybody forgot to get yesterday. I would have driven, but I thought I saw a cop go up the street a little while ago."

"Yeah, I saw him too. It was one of the new ones, a young guy who actually looked friendly," I told Jimmy. "Anyway, If you're not doing anything tonight, why don't you come over? Mom and Dad are having a party and I'm going to park the cars. I'm sure the old man wouldn't mind if you helped."

"Yeah, that sounds cool. Like what time?"

"About seven. I think."

"If you really want to be a good guy, you could finish cutting this grass ....

"Now you know one thing for sure, don't ya."

"What's that. That you're not a nice guy?" I teased, getting up from the sulky to wrap the starting rope around the fly wheel hub.

"You know you could be a detective the way you figure things out," Jimmy said getting in the last put-down.

****

Everything went according to plan. As the guests arrived Jimmy and I took their cars down the drive, parked them half on the grass and half on the road because the street was very narrow with no gravel shoulder, center line or even a curb. After we parked each car we would jog back through the woods, following the path to the top of the ridge and then to the driveway to pick up another stocker. By nine it appeared that all that were coming had arrived, so Jimmy and I surveyed the collection of cars for the one we wanted to take for a spin. We decided on a '56 Chevy stage coach with a stick shift behind a V8 power-pack engine. The car belonged to Mr. Addison who had something to do with men's clothes.

We quietly slipped our selected rod from its parking place and headed for Kathy's. In front of her house I parked at the curb and hit the horn two short ones, while teasing the gas pedal to make the engine race. It wasn't long and the porch light came on. I held my breath, hoping it wouldn't be her Mom or worse, her brother. Cool, it was Kathy. She half skipped half bounded to the driver's side, eyes wide open with excitement, pleading, "Move over and let me in."

"No, get in the other side." I wasn't giving up my seat behind the wheel to anyone. She ran around to the other door and Jimmy got out to let her sit between us.

"Aren't you afraid of getting caught and aren't you going to introduce me to your friend?"

"Oh yeah, Kathy, this is Jimmy."

"Hi, it's nice to meet you Jimmy. Now, would you do me a favor and let us have a few minutes alone please, Jimmy?"

Jimmy, with a look of rejection from behind the shock of sun bleached hair that covered his eyes, got out and started to walk up the street. Kathy turned around placing her back to the dash and pulled her bare feet up on the seat. Her breasts, straining the buttons on her tight red & white striped blouse that was tied in a knot at the middle, exposing smooth skin just above her like colored short shorts, set my heart racing. She looked like a candy cane, a very curvy and very delicious candy cane. Jimmy had hardly walked a few steps when she threw her arms around me, catching me by surprise. I couldn't turn the engine off or even take the car out of gear, so I held the brake tight and just let the clutch out slowly to stall the engine. As we hugged and kissed, I couldn't help telling her, "I love you, Kathy, can we go steady? You're... you're the, well, the most." She just sighed and hugged me tighter. I don't know how long we were going at it, but Jimmy came back, asking through the open window, "Are you two going to do this all night? Man, we've got to get this set of wheels back, if you catch my drift, dad."

I didn't care if I did thirty years to life for Grand Theft Auto. It was worth it. Kathy turned around, tugged at her blouse that had slipped around to expose the better part of a bra covered mound and said to Jimmy, "Paul and I are going steady, so please make sure he gets home safely."

I was at a loss for words as Kathy got out and ran to the house, her pony tail bouncing from side to side and top to bottom, as she yelled over her shoulder for me to call her tomorrow. I sat there not able to move, my face burning from the rush of blood. After a moment Jimmy, reached over and poked my leg saying, "Come on, man, let's roll."

Gaining composure and feeling like a real cool cat, I started the engine and we made our way out of the maze of streets and back to the main drag.

"She's pretty good lookin'. Where'd you find her?"

Trying to regain my cool so my voice would sound normal, I took my time answering. "I met her at the strip a couple of weeks ago or so."

"Maybe I should have been going to the strip instead of working all summer."

"Let's see what this thing will do," I muttered, As we passed the road home, continuing on out toward the highway.

"It's okay by me, but we've been gone over an hour already," Jimmy reminded me.

"Okay, just one run on the highway and then we'll go straight home."

We stopped at the entrance to the Lockland highway, the only completed section of divided highway that was part of the new interstate system. It was dark now with only our headlights and the traffic signal at Shepard Lane, about a mile down the road, visible. I slipped the column shift in first gear, revved the engine and let my foot slide off the clutch. The car lurched and stopped dead.

"It's a dog. I better give it more gas," I said, trying to convince Jimmy that it was the car's fault and not mine. The next time I got it right, spinning the wheels and producing a respectable fishtail which I corrected before reaching maximum RPM in first gear. At what sounded like the engine's peak, I slammed the shift lever into second and got a chirp of rubber. The feel of acceleration pushing me back into the seat was exhilarating as the car reached over eighty miles per hour before I eased it into third and backed off for the light at Shepard Lane. The light was red and I was going to peal out again when the light turned, but there was another car coming down Shepard Lane and I wanted to make sure it wasn't a cop. I did a normal take off, and once secure in my mind that the other car wasn't john-law, down shifted back into second and punched it. We were going over a hundred as we roared through the towering walls of the Highway where the pavement narrows through the heart of the suburb of Lockland. The walls, some twenty-feet high produced a neat sound as the noise of the engine and the roar of a high speed wind-whistle bounced from side to side.

Reaching the end of the four mile long highway, Jimmy who hadn't spoken, let out with the exclamation, "Jeeesus Keerrrist", as he turned up the volume on the radio to blast us with a most fitting song, "Maybellene".

Ah, the summer of '57; girls, fast cars and rock & roll music. And nothing could sum it up better than the unofficial national anthem of the time: Chuck Berry's, "Maybellene!" I mean it had everything: An untrue woman who is caught by a V8 Ford, high speed on the open road, and a beat that made you want to get up and dance. The lyrics entwined the high speed chase of a jilted lover, his overheating hot rod loosing ground until it begins to rain, in pursuit of his heart throb, Maybellene, in her Cadillac. After the rain cools his engine, the heartsick hot rodder finally catches the Caddy at the top of a hill where he wails the rhetorical questions of unfaithfulness.

The consensus was that a Cadillac, being the quality car that it was, would run a long way at a hundred miles per hour, but a Ford, even a V-8 Ford wouldn't. Hopping up a car for the quarter mile drag was one thing. But, it was entirely unrealistic to expect a hopped-up engine to stay cool at sustained high speed. The Ford had to have been a flat-head, as early overhead valve mills were dogs.

We literally lived, ate, slept, and breathed cars. We lived the lives of those depicted in the hot rod magazines and read, talked and fantasized about cars, cars and cars. We ate with axle grease impregnated fingers, while we sat on dirty garage floors and loved every minute of it. We slept and dreamed of cars and we breathed the fumes of gas and oil, burned or unburned, that were as sweet a smell to us as a Bordeaux was to a Rothschild.

****

Luck was still with us as we drove slowly up our street, past the cars we had so carefully parked a few hours earlier. Before reaching the driveway, I saw Mr. and Mrs. Addison staggering down the middle of the road. I stopped as Mr. Addison stumbled up to the window and slurred, "That's very nice of you, Paul, I was just looking for my car."

"I'm sorry I didn't realize sooner that you wanted to leave, or I would have had the car in the drive. If you want I'll turn it around for you, sir," I said, in the nicest tone of voice I could muster, my legs still shaking from the excitement of the high speed run.

"Why that's very nice of you. You're a good boy." He was so drunk he didn't notice the smell of burning rubber that permeated the car.

Summer was over, I'd be back in school, my sister Bobbi would start college next week, our father would be off on business trips and mom, as always, would be involved in some community project. Monday evening we had a leisurely family dinner. It would be a long time before we all would sit down to a meal at the same time together. Bobbi told about her class schedule and how she still needed certain credits for her English major and that John was talking marriage, but she didn't think she was ready. I saw her in a different light. Bobbi suddenly seemed older, even like more of an adult with real problems, and not so much like a sister or student. I felt more alone in the way that if I confided to Bobbi, it would be like talking to an adult, not a teenaged sister.

I could talk to Kathy if I had any problems. Who needs a sister? Kathy and I were one. It was a natural chain of events in my mind, how going steady would lead to an engagement, followed by marriage, with a home and kids. It was all so simple. Any fool could see that. I decided that I was completely happy and content and I wouldn't even look at another girl again. I squinted at Bobbi and tried to imagine if John could feel about Bobbi the way I felt about Kathy. No way. What do they know about love? Man, I was fifteen, had been in love, fought men and had driven and worked on fast cars. What could they know that I hadn't already experienced.

CHRISTMAS MIRACLE

"OUR FATHER WHO ART IN HEAVEN...." The radio station sign-off paid tribute to the eve of the birth of Christ by invoking the ageless prayer in lieu of the traditional National Anthem. At its conclusion the cab of the single-stack-Mack with-a-sleeper-on-the-back fell silent, save for the drone of the engine and rush of the wind.

Memories of his father, killed in a foxhole on a like snowy and bitter cold Christmas eve, saturated his mind. Duane Starkholder had always taken the prayer personally, wishing, hoping, believing his father was in Heaven. He was only a small boy in 1944 and had been angry that such sad news had taken the joy from his first electric train, a Lionel with pellet-induced smoking steam engine. Christmases of love brought about by time, marriage, children and now grandchildren had helped suppress remembrances of that paradoxical day and the strong feelings of another traumatic holiday.

The soon to be retired professional trucker reached for the dial in search of entertainment. Refocusing his attention on the task at hand he was surprised that over a dozen miles had been added to the mile markers during what, he thought, was a short trip down memory lane. Right now, the snow was getting heavier and he had better call home to let them know he might be a little late. He was not particularly religious, even though he believed he had witnessed a miracle - some say he was the miracle. Still he would like to be home in time for Midnight prayer service with the family.

Someday he'd show his grandsons the newspaper clippings of the Christmas of '55. He was recently married and just completing his first year with AKERS TRUCKING, driving a 1951 International 5-speed with an electric 2-speed axle. He was young, full of energy and in a hurry to spent his first Christmas with his wife. At the truck stop a few miles back he had called Barbara, his bride of ten months, only to learn that the storm had knocked out all power to their section of town and she was running low on firewood. She had said that she and the baby were sharing a sleeping bag but was scared and cold. So when the State Trooper told him they were closing the road due to the blizzard he dared the officer to try an catch him as he barreled through the road block. With chains on the tandem drive wheels and a 10,000 pound payload in the nose of the trailer he was sure nothing could stop him.

An hour and only 25 miles later he was not so sure. Some of the drifts were up to his running boards and he was tiring from the constant shifting. It seemed like every time he'd get into high 4th the tractor would slam into a drift and he'd have to double clutch the crash box down a gear usually splitting the axle at the same time. Even locating the roadway was taxing his concentration. He was fearful that the rig might jackknife, slide off the shoulder, or worse, run over the top of a stranded motorist though he hadn't seen another vehicle of any kind since the roadblock.

Spending Christmas in the cab of his truck waiting for a rescue team would be humiliating not to mention the possibility of frost bite or even death - his wife and child's! Another hour and a pitifully few miles later he was coming to believe it was going to take a miracle to get him through. Each blast of blowing snow conjured thoughts of Barbara and little David calling his name, as the kindling dwindled and the drafty old house took on the characteristics of a tomb.

Carefully, forcefully, the powerful semi rounded a bend, straining to pick up speed for the long hill into Wesson Springs. A few more turns of the wheel and he'd be warming his family even if he had to load them into this truck and find a motel.

Half way across the flat the beams from the ice encrusted head lamps bounced off a large drift in the center of the road. Failing to see a safe way around the protrusion without risking a jackknife, Duane prepared to plow through the mound. It was only at the last instant that he saw the red glow of tail lights coming from inside the mound! Cursing, double clutching and yanking the huge wheel he fought for control, clamping on the trailer brakes in a last attempt to avoid striking the car.

With a muffled thud or two the thirty-six foot trailer slipped off the shoulder dragging the cab and all hopes for a merry Christmas with it.

Dazed, but very aware of the situation, Duane scrambled into the blizzard. Illuminated only by the slowly diminishing flush of the truck's head lamps he took his bearings.

In the forested counties of Northern Minnesota night snowfall renders the surroundings virtually pitch black. There is no reflected light from distant towns and star light cannot penetrate heavy blankets of pure white pieces of dark. Realizing at once the conditions familiar to all locals, he knew he was in trouble. Before the truck lights gave out he secured a flashlight and his hooded coat and gloves from the partially overturned truck and set out to check the stalled car.

Barely audible in the blowing gale force storm, Duane could hear the cries of a man half-calling, half-praying for help. Brushing the snow from the door handle he was aware that the engine was running. In addition to the man's cries a woman's voice, or rather her moans, were filtering from the now recognizable '52 DeSoto.

Cracking open the car's door Duane inquired if everything was alright as his flashlight revealed a terrified man holding the hand of a woman, obviously about to deliver.

"Hurry up and come in, you're letting in all the cold. It must be 20 below out there and Mary Beth's about to deliver. You don't happen to be a doctor or something, do ya?" The man pleaded in run-together words.

Stuffing his large frame into the front seat of the sedan, Duane kept the light modestly trained on the ceiling, though his eyes danced between the woman's strained face and the exposed place from where another being was trying to force his or her presence. About to address the man's question the woman let out a sharp grunt gasping, "It's coming, Jake - help me, quick."

"Hold that light over here mister, please."

With the intensity of a blizzard and the softness of a snow flake a new life was brought forth on this eve of the birth of the Savior. The woman seemed to know what to do, instructing Duane where to shine the light and her husband how to tie off the cord. The moment of euphoric joy only lasted until the reality of the situation was emphatically brought to mind by the exterior conditions. But, what a moment. Amid shouts of joy, all three of them, a man, his wife, and a stranger, trapped together in a snow bound car experienced for one brief jubilant instant the hope and future of the world.

"Thanks for your light. I don't know what we would have done without it. We didn't exactly plan it this way," the man explained. "We didn't expect little, ah...Stormy, here so soon. But, Mary Beth went into labor just about the time the storm hit. Without a phone to call for help, we figured that we might be able to beat the heavy part of the snow. Our farm's only about four or five miles from here.

"Where did you come from? Do you have a car or...? Can you take us to the hospital?"

Duane explained his predicament, chagrined at his inability to keep his rig from sliding off the road.

"You're welcome to stay with us until help arrives and we're sorry about your truck and...."

"How much gas have you got?" Duane interrupted taking stock of the situation. "It might be a long time before help arrives. They closed the road. I was the last vehicle through and I had to run a road block at that."

"I guess we might have two hour's worth of fuel...closed the road? What are we going to do? A baby can't...we've been here a couple of hours already and Mary Beth's..." he spoke rhetorically in broken sentences, while the dim light of the instrument panel cast coal black shadows of Duane's figure on the roof of their snow cave.

"Well, I thank ya for the kind offer to wait out the storm here. Ordinarily I'd take you up on it, but I got a wife and child at home without any electricity and I aim to spend my Christmas keeping them warm," Duane announced.

"Besides, we can't just let "Stormy" freeze in this old car can we?"

****

"How 'bout that eastbound single-stack-Mack-with-the-sleeper-on- the-back, come-on," the CB jarred him back to the present as he automatically keyed the mic., "You got the single-stack-Mack, Kick it back, come-on."

"How's it look over your donkey? The snow's lighter the further east you go, come-on."

"You be headin' for the heart of it. That there snow be gettin' heavy in your face, come-on."

"Thanks for the update and hope you and all the other truckers listenin' to this ol' ratchet jaw has a merry one," the west bound fellow trucker exclaimed as the two cargo ships of the macadam passed in the night.

****

Maybe it was a miracle that he had been able to stumble through drifts, darkness and numbing cold, newborn bundled to his bare chest. With less than a hundred yards of open corn field, Wesson Springs General in view, his clod-hoppered right foot had found a gopher hole. Fighting to keep from falling on the baby he twisted his body enough to break his ankle. He lay there in icy pain, thoughts of his father dying in like circumstance flashing before his mind's eye. Knowing that he couldn't - wouldn't - leave his son the same way, knowing that if he didn't move it would be Spring before they found them, he forced his body to crawl. He had prayed to HIS *Father in Heaven* that night and maybe it was those prayers that got them through.

Any fool can walk, or even crawl, through a blizzard. The real miracle was the birth of Stormy. He turned out just fine, with no after effects from the ordeal. The last he'd seen this now grown man was a year ago during a visit to Los Angeles where Stormy was a Police Captain. Duane was even Godfather to Stormy's first born, Paul Duane Peterson.

The blizzard conditions that night hadn't hurt Barbara and David. They were taken in by neighbors with coal stoves. Duane would walk with a cane the rest of his life and Stormy's father lost a leg to frost bite. Mary Beth, Stormy's mother, was taken in by *Our Father* long before the rescuers came.

This night Duane didn't need any prayers, the snow slacked off and he finished his run on schedule.

Sitting next to her husband in the old downtown church pew, Barbara squeezed his hand at the sight of the lone tear that rolled down Duane's face during the closing prayer: *...thy kingdom come, thy will be done....*

CLOSE ENCOUNTERS OF THE
HEART STOPPING KIND

KA-POW, KA-POW, KA-POW the sound of the .357 Magnum reverberated off the walls of the combination workshop, garage and machine shop. I reached for the remote to terminate the inane slaughter of television violence.

I usually kept the TV on while working on the Sedan Delivery, if for no other reason than to mask expletives and cries of pain whenever I pinched a pinky. The reason for the elaborate workshop was the '57 Chevy, my pride and joy. The ground-up restoration that had begun over three years ago was now nearing completion. I was attending to the final details at a leisurely pace just to drag the time out as long as possible. The real fun being, working on the project. This former rust heap was now a very stock, prim and proper delivery truck complete with "Wilson's Meat Market" painted on the sides. Even the engine was stock, albeit hardly an engine that the corner beef and pork shop would order - a 283 cubic inch, 283 horsepower fuel injected mill.

Killing the fluorescent overheads and their incessant hum brought deafening quiet as I closed up for the night. Now the only sound to penetrate the solitude of our secluded haven on the shores of Goose Creek Bay, was that of a Great Horned Owl and the light rustling of leaves from the wisps of a soft summer breeze.

Complacency and tranquillity could only describe my feelings as I stepped onto the deck surrounding this picture-windowed cedar home, nestled among the trees of our 144 acre Hoosier farm. Admiring the view across the Ohio of the Kentucky hills with its smattering of manmade lights, the only visible illumination, I walked the length of the deck to our bedroom.

After undressing in preparation to shower, I moved back outside to gather some towels that had been left to dry on the rail earlier in the day. Turning to retrace the two steps to the bedroom's sliding-screen door, I was stunned to see the outline of a man, his feet firmly planted, standing halfway down the deck. A quick glance was all I needed to see that this invader of placidity was about my size, had heavy, bushy, dark hair and...AND he had something in his hand, and that something, was pointing at me!

Having been a police officer and a private investigator I've been in tight spots before, but standing naked on my own property, this guy really got my attention! With my eyes riveted on the thing leveled at me I screamed at him, "WHO ARE YOU...GET OUT OF HERE," as I struggled to reach the door. He didn't say anything and as best I could see his expressionless blank stare didn't change.

Stumbling, crashing, running into the house, slamming the screen door closed behind me, I saw out of the corner of my eye, that the trespasser was now advancing toward my end of the deck. The thoughts that went through my mind as I raced to the bureau where I kept a gun, ran from..."This must be a friend playing a joke on me and he's going to burst out laughing any second," to..."this could only be a sleaze bag from some past arrest or investigation

who had sworn to get me."

In what seemed like an inordinate amount of time, I reached the dresser - hang on now - just give me half a second. The muscles in my back tensed in preparation for the bullet that was sure to come as my brain struggled to scan all enemies, past and present.

Snatching the pistol from a drawer full of socks, I whirled around, dropped to the floor behind the bed and came up with the classic two-hand hold directed at the screen door whose frame was now filled by the stranger. The silent stranger with something in his hand.

Again I yelled for the man to leave or tell me what he wanted or who he was, anything. No response. He just stood there in the shadows while the harsh incandescence light from the bathroom spotlighted me. Now I could detect that the ominous object in his hand had something sticking out of it - like a barrel!

I waited, listening, looking for the flash of fire that was surely only moments away. Maybe the screen will deflect the bullet, maybe he'll miss, maybe.... The years of police indoctrination took hold as I resigned myself to empty my gun into this intruder before I died. I strained to see, almost hoping to discern a flash of fire that would bring this confrontation to a very climatic and final end. My death threat didn't move, didn't make a sound. The screen rippled. It might have been the wind. The hair on the back of my neck stood up.

I had to think, go over my options, form a plan, I couldn't take my eyes off the thing in his hand. Surely this isn't real - too much TV!

Events were now moving in slow motion as I recognized the onset of tachyinterval - the phenomena that occurs when under extreme stress events seen to be happening in slow motion. I didn't have to shoot unless he shot first or unless I was sure it was a weapon he was holding and he gave some indication that he was going to use it. Since I was home alone I could even allow him to enter the house, and as long as he didn't try to get too close or actually assault me, I could just play this thing out. I really wanted to know who he was...and, why?

The bed I was behind afforded enough cover that I didn't want to risk trying for the phone to call the sheriff or a neighbor - the nearest being over a half mile to the west. Besides the police would be at least 20 minutes away since there was only one on-duty officer for the entire county. I could make a dash for the hallway where I could hide, but if he shot me as I ran I wouldn't be able to return the favor. Besides he could hide too and wait until I went to bed or my wife and sons came home and then attack.

Half lying, half sitting, still undressed, light shining on me and my legs beginning to cramp I continued to shout, "WHO ARE YOU... WHAT DO YOU WANT...GET OUT OF HERE OR I'LL BLOW YOU AWAY, MAN!"

My imagination was running wild. Maybe he was just guarding the door so the real perp could slip in the front and sneak up behind me. I tried to be cognizant of my peripheral vision lest I take my eyes from what has to be some form of lethal and instant destruction hidden by the screen. I held my breath so not even the sound of my breathing could mask another invader.

Then, still without so much as a word, he turned and started back down the deck. In a flash I killed the light in the bathroom and pulled on a pair of shorts then ran toward the hall. I don't know why I took the time to put on my briefs, but it made me feel better, less vulnerable.

Reaching the entrance way, I saw through the kitchen window, that he had reached the end of the deck. He froze as I covered him with light from the driveway floods while opening the door and taking careful aim. He was less than twenty feet from me now and I could see what was in his hand. It was a pencil and pad of paper.

He could have been killed. I might have shot him. My head felt hot and at the same time a chill came over my whole body. I'd had men in my sights before, but this was different. I was just doing my job then, this was personal - this was my home!

I motioned for him to come over where he displayed a message on the pad reading, "My Father says I'm a very special person". The stranger was a mentally handicapped, deaf mute!

Keeping my distance I put the gun down and took his pad. After writing notes back and forth he finally told me who he was. He seemed shy, so I invited him in the kitchen for a Coke while I telephoned his family who promised to send someone right up. I learned from further note writing that he had often admired our house from the road and just wanted to see it up close. He had driven his car only part way up the quarter mile driveway, with his lights out, and had walked the rest of the way.

End of story? Not quite. The next day I learned that he was a walk-away from a state mental hospital, committed by his family because he was prone to violence and had attacked people during previous encounters. On this occasion he had savagely beaten his aged father before stealing the car he used to visit me. His brother told me the family wouldn't have held it against me if I had killed him.

I was relieved that the taking of a human life hadn't been necessary, but I was also comforted that I had subscribed to the old country adage: "The door might not always be locked, but the gun is always loaded". Maybe he had wanted more than just a look, but the gun scared him. What if the gun hadn't been available or what if the kids or my wife had been home and one of them had been the first to encounter him, what if....

THE DETECTIVE

The piercing light was visible long before he heard the two longs followed by two shorts as the Chicago bound James Whitcomb Riley approached the Canal Street crossing. Within minutes the E-9, the most powerful of diesel engines was thundering into Winton Place station. Though the little two piece windshield, just aft of the giant single head lamp, towered over his head he couldn't suppress the smile and memory of last week's Christmas. Then it was he who towered over an E-9, a Lionel with "Santa Fe" splashed in orange and silver across the side of his gift to his wide eyed nephew.

From his vantage point, near the Western Union window, Kurt Kidwell, could see the platform to the right and the parking lot to his left.

The target was nowhere to be found. Maybe Miss Dolly had set him up, given him a bum steer, and they were traveling by car. He watched, ticket in hand, as the porters loaded and unloaded boxes, grips, trunks and all sizes of suitcases. He watched the passengers embark and disembark, especially the smart looking tan-suited knockout with the matching hat perched atop her stacked honey blond hair. Kidwell never took his eye off the lot. Maybe he was already on-board having caught the train at the Oakley Station.

The man who earned a living watching, watched, with a sinking feeling, as the Brakeman, lantern in hand, got into position at the rear of the train. It had begun to rain. Kidwell stepped toward the Pullman car, Starlight, as the sound of tires straining for adhesion on gravel commanded his attention. Caught in the head lamps of the a dirty black '49 Cadillac convertible, the trademark of Mr. Pogue, Kidwell pulled the brim of his fedora a little lower and the collar of his trench coat up as he stepped onto the Starlight's platform.

The Brakeman began to move his lantern up and down, the signal for the engineer to get underway. Mr. Pogue and his driver, laden with two suitcases and a string tied cardboard box, had to be helped onto the now moving train by the Brakeman.

He'd give Pogue an hour or so then he'd look him up. He wasn't going anywhere for at least a few hours - the Riley's first stop. Right now Kidwell needed the men's room and some warm food. Entering the day- coach, El Capitan, he searched the overhead racks for a place to stash his hat and coat. Amid leather suitcases, paperboard composite grips and round ladies' hat boxes with the name of swank department stores emblazoned on the richly colored Chrome-Kote wrapping, he found an unobtrusive spot. The car's seats were filled more with small trunks, a few leather trimmed canvas covered grips and gift boxes than the holiday travelers themselves. Tossed on and between were an array of coats and outer wear, a leather flyer's jacket, a smartly creased gentleman's felt hat with a tweed sport jacket and a hangered sailor's dress blues. The lavatory was clean, properly stocked and a great relief.

The dining car was about half full so Kidwell had no trouble settling into a starched linen covered table, complimented with a small bouquet of fresh flowers snugged against the window. Within a minute the hospital-white clad waiter filled Kidwell's order for a Jack Daniels on the rocks. Complacency settled over the Private Investigator as he casually observed soothed couples' happy faces reflected by the individual table lamps against their personal half-shaded windows. They dined on choice Prime Rib, Boursin Chicken or Stuffed Lemon Sole as America's backyards roll by. The dressed to the nines, tan-suited knockout, smiled at him over the top of a tall cold exotic something. Kurt Kidwell discretely adjusted his shoulder holster before approaching tan-suit.

"I'm Karl Kinder, may I join you?" he asked, athletically jostling his muscular body into the opposite seat as the train rocked over a set of switches. The pseudo name was one he used when dealing with strangers while on the job. In this business, you never know who's also on the job on the opposite side.

"Seems that you already have, and I'm happy to meet you, I think. My name is Victoria and that, that drunken soldier who just came in has been bothering me. Uh, oh, here he comes again."

"Well...there you are little lady. I thought I lost ya. Is thesh man bothering you," the three-stripe non-com slurred.

"I think it's the other way around, Sergeant. The lady is with me so please refrain from interfering with us again, Kurt said, in a kind manner, rising from his seat while boring his eyes into a set of slightly dilated pupils.

It was really all one move, the words, the stare and the arm lock that crumpled the uniform to his knees. Reducing the pressure enough to allow the intruder to be half dragged, Kidwell deposited the rude soldier in the forward sleeper admonishing him to sleep it off.

Returning to his upholstered dinner table chair beneath the car length, hand-painted mural covering the frieze on both sides of the older 1937 era dining car, the lady named Victoria smiled again, "Thank you ever so much, Mr. Kinder." The soft pastel colors highlighted by the hanging globe lights lent an aura of mystic and intrigue to this calm and sophisticated lady.

During the interlude that preceded the main course the widowed heir to an old manufacturing company and the gentleman with the clandestine demeanor, discretely exchanged pleasantries.

They dined on filet mignon with sautéed mushrooms and fresh spinach au gratin. When the plates had been cleared they sipped Three Star Henessey as winking roadside crossings lights occasionally flashed across the darkened window. He told her his business was corporate acquisitions and he, also, was on his way home to Chicago.

The train, now at cruising speed of seventy plus, set up a gentle rocking motion which, between cars as he was seeing her to her bedroom compartment, caused her to fall into him. He steadied her, feeling firm upper arms and catching a scent of Channel Number Five. They stood close to let another passenger pass. The vibes oozed. "I've got some business to take care of," he said, locking into her light green eyes. "If I stop back in an hour or so can we have a night cap?"

She returned his gaze before twisting, brushing against his arm, as she unlocked the door, "I'd like that. I need to freshen up a little, anyway."

Since Pogue hadn't visited the dining car he had to be between there and the club car. Kidwell set out to scout the train. The top half of the outside door to the car just ahead of the lounge car was open, a fact noted by the PI in case anything had to be tossed out. Stepping into the club car, an older model with a half length mahogany bar down one side, Kidwell smiled to the lone bartender as his eyes scanned the room. Seated in the fore section was a businessman studying a newspaper next to his young, comic book reading son and a fidgeting, beer drinking sailor. Halfway back, Mr. Pogue, holding the twine tied box, and his chauffeur were complacently sipping cocktails. Kidwell walked the length of the room, surreptitiously verified the door to the observation platform was unlocked, and sat at the rear most table. The bartender looked up but the private dick shook his head while picking up a Life magazine.

He didn't like the situation. He didn't like all the witnesses. He didn't like the driver, if that's what he really was. If he was a driver, then why did he leave the Caddy at the train station and why did he keep looking around - like a body guard. The diesel horn sounded, two longs followed by two shorts for the approach of a public crossing. The now tense six foot P.I. had been counting since the first. The engineer had been very punctual. Almost exactly eleven seconds after the first blast of the horn the sound of the crossing bells reached the last cars on the train. The bells and their flashing red lights bouncing through the train's windows was quite distracting.

The sailor got up to leave, the P.I. started another magazine. It didn't look like Pogue was in any hurry by the number of olive pits in the ash tray. Body guard was sipping something dark with ice through a straw - probably a Coke if he was on the job. He had hoped to have concluded the business by now, but there had been too many people and he hadn't counted on a body guard.

The job had seemed simple enough when the phone call came, followed by the packet of cash and instructions. All he had to do was trade the package Mr. Pogue was to be carrying for the cash Kurt was carrying in his inside jacket pocket. He was instructed to secure the package at all costs, something about a threat to national security. It seemed his clientele only called when the job was too tough or sticky for lesser agents.

When the executive and his son rose to leave, Kurt signaled the bartender. He asked the practiced elderly Negro if he would be so kind as to check with the kitchen for an order of cheese and crackers. Now there were only three.

"Mr. Pogue, I'd like a word...."

"Mr. Pogue don't talk to nobody, so take a powder, pal," the burly body guard belched forcing his way between them.

Time was short before the barkeep or another passenger would walk in. Kidwell lowered his eyes and turned slightly to send body language messages of capitulation while he searched for words to stall for time and a piece of luck. Softly he began, "I'm sorry sir, I didn't mean to intrude it's only that...the words were lost to the wail of the E-9's horn...won't bother...eight - nine - ten - the bells clanged, the lights flashed, the bruiser's concentration broke as he looked out the windows. Just like the sergeant, and so many others before him, it was all one move. The P.I.'s foot found the male tender spot just below the belly button an instant before the right hand connected with the jaw of the stunned and buckling galoot.

Mr. Pogue, impaired by the martinis could only stare, slack jawed, as Kurt dragged the unconscious body through the rear doors and onto the observation platform. The thought of tossing the dead weight over was tempting, but he had confidence that his body guarding days were over for the night.

"Now then, Mr. Pogue, before we were so rudely interrupted we have business to transact. I have here," Kidwell began extracting the envelope filled with cash from his jacket pocket, "A large sum of money that I intend to trade you for the box on your lap."

"What have you done with Bruno. It's not for sale, now please leave me or I shall summon the authorities. Bartender, bartender...."

"I sent him away, it's just you and me. Time is short and you only have two choices."

"What do you mean? Who are you? I'm not selling. All you and your kind want to do is keep it off the market. My invention will...."

As the inventor rambled on, Kidwell took the man's half drained highball from the table top and casually tossed it into his face. The slightly intoxicated keeper of the box reacted before he

153

realized he had relaxed his grip on the box. That was all the practiced P.I. needed. He flipped the envelope on the table and strode out, catching out of the corner of his eye, the opening platform door and the guard struggling in, revolver in hand!

"Is it a present for me?" the golden-haired lady impishly chided as she opened the door at his knock. "Or is it a reward from rescuing other maidens?"

His face relaxed and a smile spread to his dimples as he surveyed the room and the silk robe clad lady. But his mind was racing. "Sorry to put you to any trouble, but I'm in a bit of a jam and I might need your help."

He put the box down on the day couch, turned to look her in the eye to see if she was with him. She held her head high and stared back at him. He took her squared shoulders in his powerful hands pulling her toward him. It was a closed mouth kiss, he afraid of relaxing, and she, just to let him know the quid pro quo was sealed.

He told her that the box contained medical experiments that a Russian agent, an armed Russian agent on board the train, was trying to steal from him. "Look, I think the train is going to stop soon and when it does I'll need you to get off with me. They won't be looking for a couple, especially one with glasses," he said producing a pair of eye glasses with clear lenses.

It didn't take long before the sound of the thug could be heard in the passage way, banging on every door. There wasn't time to discuss anything.

Bang, bang, bang, "Open the door."

Slowly she opened the door a crack. The bully, gun in hand, pushed, slamming it against the closet. "What's the meaning of this...."

"Shut up. Where is he?"

"How dare you. There's no one in here. Who...." He pushed passed her, looking first toward the beds then at the toilet room door.

Kidwell, crouched, back to the wall, in the tiny, crowded, pitch- black room, eased his HSc Mauser out of the shoulder holster and leveled it at the door. Over the click-clack of the train's wheels he heard the distinct click of the door handle as the Mauser's safety clicked off.

Having killed before and in control of the situation, fear was absent, though he was, maybe a mite apprehensive. The little 7.65 pocket pistol, taken from a Nazi officer he had garroted during his days in the service of his country, was a favorite of his arsenal of concealable weapons. Its reliability had been established in past operations.

BlaaaaaaaaaaaaCrack,Crack,Crackaaaaaaaat. The timing of the diesel locomotion's announcement that it was approaching a station couldn't have been more opportune.

The aggressor, dumbfounded at the three thirty-two caliber crimson holes in his shirt front, paradoxically glimpsed the lavatory mirror for his final vision - the face of a dead man.

"Victoria, Victoria give me a hand, he's fallen on me."

The previously formal and composed lady Victoria, ashen and wide eyed, nonetheless dutifully stepped over the body and extended a hand.

"Get dressed and put on some lipstick, we're getting off here." She stood there, gaping at the body as the impact of the situation began to sink in. Struggling with her suit case, he slapped her hard on the rump, "get moving, NOW!"

With the smaller of her two suitcases he dumped their contents on the bed, placed the string tied box inside, and packed what he could of the dumped contents around the box.

"What we can't get into your other suitcase, I'll replace," he stated, throwing undergarments and personal items into the larger grip as the train slowed for the station stop.

Victoria, displaying genuine aristocratic style, smiled as she accompanied the P.I. through the El Capitan where he retrieved his hat and coat. As a cold wind whipped at their ankles they snuck across the platform to a waiting cab.

The hotel in this out-of-the-way little burg was, if nothing else, a safe haven. Here, as the lady bathed, he inspected the contents of the box he had killed for.

After his shower, and standing in his under shorts, he moved to take her into his arms, "I just want to hold you."

"You mean gratuitously? For helping you conduct whatever dirty business you're in? Perhaps you better tell who you really are, Mr. Karl Kinder, if that's your real name." She had regained her full stature as a business executive. "You have presented yourself as a gentleman, at least in your dealings with me. Please continue to do so. I have no intention of allowing this room to become a tryst."

"I understand and respect your wishes. All I said was I wanted to hold you. I need a little tenderness now and I thought you might also."

"Who are you? What...."

"It's best that you don't know my real name. I'm a private investigator and sometimes my assignments get a little ah...hairy. I'm sorry to have involved you in this, but making use of you as cover, seemed like a good idea at the time. After this matter is concluded I'd like to try to start all over - on a social level, especially since we're both from Chicago. Right now I think we both could use a little, make that a lot, of TLC.

She came to him. They hugged. The tension dissipated. In a short while they fell asleep.

Around nine he slipped out, paid the hotel bill and, box in hand, wolfed down a pancake breakfast at a greasy spoon two blocks down the street. Finding himself in the seedier part of town he quickly located a pawn shop where he purchased a used canvas suitcase in which to carry the box.

He caught a cab to the station, bought a ticket on the next train to Chicago and found a public telephone. Three rings and he heard his client, "Consolidated Gas and Oil, Incorporated, may I help you?" the sweet voice of a young operator answered.

"Extension 447, Please"

" Yes."

"This is Kidwell."

"Have you got it?"

"Yes sir."

"Where are you? Tell me what's in the box."

"I'm a couple of hours out of the LaSalle Street Station. The box contains a lot of diagrams, blue prints and legal papers plus what looks like a carburetor - a special kind of carburetor."

"Excellent. Come directly to the Drake. We will meet you in the lobby."

He had a half hour to kill before departure. Maybe he could find a little something for Miss Dolly. She had really come through for him, but the thoughts of a special lady is what was really twisting around in his mind. He took a walk around the block, past a Negro bar where he stopped to listen to a solo cornetist crying some blues number that drifted by like a spirit on the winds of time.

Author's note: *Rumors have circulated for at least half a century that a man named Pogue (or Fish or ???) invented a carburetor that produced unprecedented fuel economy. The rumor includes the scenarios that the petroleum producers, foreign interests and/or the automobile manufacturers, to keep the product off the market, stole the design and to keep Mr. Pogue/Fish/??? quiet, paid him off or....*

THE ALUMNI

Yeah, we were there in the beginning
singing, dancing and spinning,
driving, racing and winning.
To make those days our own,
to make our mark, to set us apart,
then suddenly we were grown.

"Roland, I don't know if you've met Joel, and I'm sorry to have to throw you two together with such short notice, but time on this project is of the essence," the Vice President of Engineering stated in a friendly business tone. "Maybe you two can get acquainted at lunch. Your backgrounds are similar so I'm sure you guys will get along just fine," the veep continued, hurrying out the door, secretary and assistant in tow.

"I just signed on with the firm last month and I still can't keep pace with that man. I hope you work a little slower," Joel sighed out loud extending his hand to Roland.

"Well, maybe just a little. You'll get used to it." Roland smiled happily sizing up his new partner's firm hand shake and sincere eye contact. He spread the blueprints on the layout table relieved that his request for help on the project had been answered.

They worked through lunch finally breaking around 4:00 PM but not before committing to at least four more hours of work after a good meal.

The typical Southern California summer day - warm, breezy and comfortable, allowed the men to dine at one of La Jolla's many outdoor cafes. Roland often took a late lunch finding the empty restaurants of the mid-afternoon quiet and unhurried.

It took a beer and the better part of an hour before the men could put the project out of their mind and conversation. Sipping a foam topped Coors, Roland, relaxed and finally enjoying the company, offered, "I'm from the Midwest, born in '41, divorced, two kids - both grown. My only hobby, aside from work, is reading about what I used to love to do and still might do again - build fast cars. What about you? You look to be about the same age."

"Thanks for the compliment. I'm four years your senior, still married to my high school sweetheart, two grown daughters and also used to play around with fast cars, but that was back when I was a kid in high school. Oh yeah, I'm also from the Midwest, Cincinnati to be exact."

"Cincinnati?" Roland said it with surprise and delight as a big smile crossed his weather lined face. "It sure is a small world. I was born and raised in that river city. Got my start in hot rodding in the Cam Lifters car club. What's your last name? Surely we know some of the same people."

The Drifters, The Platters,
Diana and the girls,
who sang the songs of our soul.
Pony tails and fender skirts
and BABY LET THE GOOD TIMES ROLL.

"Cam Lifters, eh?" A grin forming on Joel's tanned face. "Why you cats and greasers never could build hot cars if ya dig what I mean, daddy-o," the vernacular of the fifties slipping into Joel's ribbing. "You must have known Denny...what's-his-name. Had a V8-60 in a chopped and channeled deuce coupe. Oh yeah. My last name is Cassidy. What's yours?"

"Cassidy? I know you or rather I remember you, an upperclassman, member of the Knights and had the '53 Ford that beat Tommy Ivinski's '57 Plymouth Fury. Man, they talked about that race for years. You were a few years ahead of me at Woodward High but everyone knew who you were. Oh wow! I idolized you back then. This is going to be a great project." Like high speed pistons they pumped each other with questions about past times and people...whatever happened to Paul Auer, Jack Cambry, Isky and....?

"I think Paul Auer joined the club about the time I quit to go to college. He built a sports car with a fiberglass body, didn't he? I don't know whatever happened to Isky, but I heard that Jack Cambry hooked up, again, with the little red head who drove a '55 Chev. He used to drive a Vette and now she's the one with the Vette. My wife is the former Amy Levine, class of '60. Did you know her? What about you, what'd you drive?'

"Oh wow. I knew her. She was in the same class as Auer. I remember them both. she was some looker, a cheerleader as I remember. Boy some guys have all the luck," Roland complimented his new friend from the past as memories exploded inside the combustion chamber of his mind. "I was a Chevy man. My first car was a used '55 two-door sedan that I bought in 1960 for $500, blown-up engine and all. I overhauled the little V8 and drove it in its stock state for two years. Actually it wasn't all that stock. I bored it out, reworked the four barrel and slipped in a McGurk 3/4 cam and installed larger intake valves - from the Chevy six cylinder Powerglide - if I remember correctly. That set-up got me a lot of trophies at the ol' Beechmont Drag Strip. I'd have kept right on with my little "stocker" if I hadn't been protested."

Ricky Nelson and Jackie Wilson,
Little Richard and Jerry Lee,
Hootenannies and SHORT FAT FANNIE
and OH, OH TRAGEDY.
THE STROLL and THE STOMP
and AT THE HOP, TWISTIN' THE NIGHT AWAY,
South Philly and Bo Diddley,
rock and roll was here to stay

"How'd you get caught?" Joel asked, as memories of fast cars and other fabulous fifties memorabilia crowded his current engineering project for brain space.

"I guess I just got a little too cute. I put a set of Inglewood cheater slicks on the bomb. They were recaps and looked like regular tires, white walls and all, except they were softer and didn't have any tread. The guys in the inspections lane almost never looked at tire tread so I thought I'd chance it. I got through the inspections okay, but faster times on the fastest "C" Stock car drew the attention of a few of the others and they caught me. I was banned from the strip for the rest of the year so I spent that time building for Gas class."

Tossing down the last of his beer, Roland checked his Rolex, grinned, then signaled the waitress. "This is great fun but we really have to finish the project. Tell ya what. Let's have another cold one, swap a few more lies and then promise to work at least until midnight. Okay, Joel?"

Nodding his drink order to the waitress, Joel picked up on Roland's soul baring. "And I thought I was the only one who, uh...shall we say, resorted to unconventional and questionable methods. Everybody thought that little flathead was stock except for the duals and twin Stromberg 92's. Man that little convertible sported a Vic Hubbard 3/8 stroker kit, a .060 over-bore, a Potvin three-eight cam, 4.11 gears, milled head and of course a complete port, polish and relief job. An unpainted and dirty engine with a stock looking head fooled everyone including Tommy Ivinski and his push-button Henry-J. When I sold it a few years later, to some college frat brother, I don't even think I told him what was in it. Of course by then I had reinstalled the stock single carb and manifold and reinstalled the stock rear gears to improve the gas mileage. Boy, those were some times. It didn't take much to be a winner: an extra carb or two, dual exhausts and a fine tune job plus a little help on the outside."

Do you remember GOOD GOLLY MISS MOLLY,
Chuck Berry and Buddy Holly,
Three-twos and spinner caps,
drive-ins and glass packs,
James Dean and YAKETY-YAK
and a screamin' tenor sax.

"Speaking of tune-ups. One of the best known secrets...say what did you mean by, outside help?"

"I don't think I ever told anyone this. Let me think and remember for a minute. Go ahead and finish what you were about to say about tune- ups," Joel promised.

"Okay, but no holding back. I was just recalling that one of the best little known secrets was the GM publication, <u>CORVETTE NEWS</u>. As I remember it was only a quarterly magazine but they published the factory specs for race tuning the Vette engine. If you bought a Vette new they put you on their mailing list. I don't think you could buy it or get a subscription. It was only for new Vette owners but the mag was always available at the local Chevrolet dealer. Most guys spent endless hours and time trials in an attempt to gain peak performance when some of us just used the free factory information. Chevrolet, in the early years of their racing era, were most helpful to hot rodders. Maybe that's why I'm still a Chevy man."

"How'd you happen to become an engineer? And what other racing have you been involved in?" Joel asked, still excited about finding an ex- Cincinnati hot rodder, some 2000 odd-miles from home, for a working partner.

"Well, just after I graduated from high school, I got a job with Cincinnati Milling Machine in their apprentice program. I earned my degree at UC at night and worked days at the Mill. My free time I spent building the old '55 with the new larger and higher revving 283. I threw away those cheater slicks and got the real thing, Bruce slicks. To the engine I added a Chet Herbert Roller Cam and topped the whole thing off with a Latham vane-type blower. Naturally, the inside work included porting, polishing, flycutting and balancing. All of the machine work was done on the sly at the Mill. The little two-door really cranked. At its best, with the spider gears welded together and 4.56 ring & pinion, it ran just over 108 in just under thirteen seconds." My only other racing has been through my kids when they were growing up. We went through a bunch of go-karts. Now tell me about this deep dark secret."

"It's really no big deal. It's just that the night I raced Tommy we filled his tank with white gas," Joel confessed.

"You mean the stuff we used to run in our lawn mowers. The stuff that didn't contain lead and was very low octane?" Roland interrupted.

"Yeah, that's the stuff. One of the other Knights poured a few gallons into Tommy's Fury while I made sure Tommy stayed inside Carter's. When I got the signal that the deed was done I started a put-down about how Plymouths were dogs. Tommy, in the middle of trying to put the make on that little blonde waitress that everybody had the hots for, fell for the goad. I never did like him and his know-it-all attitude.

"We pulled right out on Reading Road to smoke one off. He had me by at least half-a-car in first, but by the time I slapped second gear the impotent gas must have gotten to his engine because I just flew by. We then went down the Lockland Highway, and from a roll at about forty or so, cranked one off again. I left him in the dust.

"Not being much of a mechanic he couldn't tell what was wrong, only that his Fury didn't run as well as he thought it should. By the time he had run through the gas in his tank and refueled a day or so later the car was running fine again. He told some of the guys that the reason he lost was that his plugs were fouled. He spread the word around that there was going to be a re-match, but I ignored it - everybody knew the flathead was fast. I don't think that no-clubber ever hung out at Carter's again."

The two men, well into their middle years, reminisced late into the evening secure in the knowledge that to this bygone era they truly belonged.

In the beginning those times were ours
the words, the music, the clothes and the cars,
hot rods and puppy love
and guardian angels up above.

TEXAS/NEW MEXICO, 1961

The sun has riz,
and the sun has set,
and we ain't outta Texas yet

The big square trademark radiator filled my outside rearview mirror. He looked like he was going to run over the top of me - and I was running 90 miles per hour! The dark blob in my mirror had been gaining on me for at least the past fifteen minutes. At first I thought it was a cop, but the rate he was closing was steady and not increasing as if it were the police. Besides, 90 was not really considered speeding west of San Antonio. Speed limit signs were seldom encountered and actual "speed limits" were, in many parts of the west were what ever was "reasonable and proper."

I had left Houston early that morning with limited funds advanced by the Show Winds Theatrical Company. It was summer, 1961, I was nineteen and had started a dream job as the front man for a live stage show company that produced one-night stands in small towns across the southwest. My first stop-over was Pecos.

I edged closer to the berm and again checked my instruments: Tach, 4000, engine temperature 185°, oil pressure.... It was a huge silver and black Rolls Royce and it was now abreast of me. The mustachioed driver, black cap atop his head, didn't even acknowledge me while the passenger, in the rear seat, couldn't be seen from behind the newspaper he was reading.

This is not happening. This is Texas, USA, and I'm driving the most powerful American car made - the 1960 Corvette! I can't let this happen - this is for the honor of America. I fed a little more fuel to my three Rochester, two-barrel carburetors and matched the interlopers speed - 110. After a few minutes in his slipstream, I moved over into the east bound lanes and shoved my foot in it. The little roadster responded with push-you-back-in-the-seat acceleration while the twin straight-through mufflers resonated off the side of the Rolls. I topped out at a little over 125 and then settled back to 120 - a nice easy two-mile-per-minute clip. I gleefully watched the Rolls growing smaller in my mirrors.

It was hot, maybe 90 or so, and even the rush of air at such a high speed didn't help much. My cheerfulness quickly faded upon glancing at my gauges. The engine temperature was approaching 220 degrees! I had removed the thermostat prior to beginning the trip knowing the little 283 engine would need all the advantages it could get in the hot south-west summer. The engine was basically the 270 horsepower version to which I had exchanged the two-four barrel carbs for three-deuces on straight linkage. The reason was for better response during high speed cornering and improved fuel economy - it got 14.5 MPG at a cruising speed of 90 per. Other attributes included metallic brake linings, quick steering, 4- speed transmission, heavy duty shocks and a 3.70 rear axle.

I had been running all day at 90 without straining the engine, but the extra 30 MPH had been too much. I cut back down to 90. Sure enough, 15 minutes later here came the Rolls with the haughty chauffeur and oblivious passenger - 110, steady as she goes. Well, we don't have to tell anyone - obviously they won't - they didn't even know they had slighted an American icon.

Hot, dirty, tired and coming down with a cold, I stopped at a Pecos hospital where I conned the resident into giving me a shot of penicillin. Then twelve hours in an air conditioned cabin at Jim Bob's & Mary Beth's Tourist Haven and I was ready to begin work. The agreement was, I was to deliver and post bills in common places of the city. I was also to visit any and all local radio stations and newspapers with publicity releases and offer interviews. Posting the flyers was without incident. However, the radio stations and the only local newspaper were reluctant to give me an interview or a promise to plug the upcoming show.

I was allowed two days to complete my work before moving on to the next town. At each town the Company was to have waiting for me a money order, care of general delivery. On the morning of the third day there was still no letter at the post office. I called Houston and was told some long tale that I should not worry they'll make it up to me in Farmington, New Mexico, the next scheduled town. Boy, was I naive. They didn't send me out completely without support. They gave me $30.00 for gas money, which, at .20/gallon was good for about 900 miles.

Around noon the next day, I rolled into Roswell just as a local parade was mustering on the main drag. I flopped the top and, hand waving to the crowds like I was one of the floats, got into line behind what turned out to be the mayor's car - a '61 Chevy Convertible. About the time the parade got to the center of town, a motorcycle cop pulled along side of me, signaling that I should follow him. Oops. At the police station, I tried to tell them I was just following traffic when I some how got mixed up with the parade vehicles. That was almost truthful inasmuch as a cop, way back at the beginning, asked me if I was in the parade and I nodded yes. Since they couldn't get the mayor to forgo his parade and ceremonial affair to hear my case, the sergeant ordered that I be escorted out of town. Next stop, Route 66 and Albuquerque for dinner and a night's sleep.

The next day, I gassed up and inquired of the best route to Farmington. The locals at the gas station, while admiring my car and asking if I was on the Route 66 TV show, advised I should stay on 66 to Gallup and turn north there as the roads running north out of Albuquerque to the four-corners area were not all paved. I didn't tell them I was on the show, but I didn't tell them I wasn't, either. On my way out of town, I noticed I had picked up a few followers - kids from the gas station who had tried to goad me into a race. The leader of the pack, driving a maroon 1957 Chevrolet with louvers on the hood, lowering blocks and a shaved nose and deck, kept riding up on my rear bumper. Once or twice, when traffic permitted, he pulled along side, shoved it into second gear and goosed it a few times while his shotgun called for a race. After a few miles of this, the taunts and threats became abusive and it was clear I needed to do something.

Picking a stretch of Highway 66 that looked to have a sharp curve at the end of a short straightaway, I changed down into third and opened the throttle full. The '57, taken by surprise, lagged a hundred feet back by the time I had entered the hard right hand turn. One of the other attributes I added to my Vette was a switch panel that included switches for my brake lights, tail lights, left tail light, four-way-flasher (not a factory option yet) and under-hood lights. The tail light switch was in case I was being followed, at night, by someone I didn't want to catch me - such as a cop. I could turn out the tail lights making it very hard for him to see me. The left tail light switch was for the same purpose, whereas if a cop was chasing a car with two tail lights, but after a few hills and dales between us, the only car in front of him had one tail light, he would think the car he was chasing had turned off. It did work, but that's another story.

Hurtling down the highway at close to 90, and with the '57 coming on strong, things got very busy. Just before trouncing the binders, I flipped the switch canceling the brake lights. With a quick heal-toe maneuver I jammed the shift lever into second gear red-lining the engine. The car shuttered as the speed dropped. Tires howling in protest, I induced an under-steer setting up a four wheel drift. As the right front tire, just over the edge of the pavement and on the dirt berm fought for adhesion, and just before the apex, I poured the coal to her while straightening the wheel to compensate for drift. Once clear of the corner, I stole a glance at my rear view mirror. The Chevy driver, obviously thinking that if I could take the corner without braking, he could too - learned to late something wasn't right. I couldn't see exactly what happened, but there was a lot of dust and I never saw them again.

Farmington was void of any hotels or motels, but I did find a nice home that offered rooms to rent - $3.00 per night including breakfast and dinner. That was after I checked the post office - no mail here either. I couldn't help being an optimist; my mother was a Pollyanna. I began the next day calling on the local radio station. Here, a kindly, older DJ/station manager took pity on me and told me how, after the town had been excited about and helped promote the theatrical company's promise to come last year - never showed up. When, I told him of how I hadn't been paid he offered to treat me to dinner at his lodge in Durango, Colorado.

The 60 mile trip through the mountains to this old west town, nestled down into a valley amid jagged mountain peaks, was the most beautiful scenery I had ever seen. The "one dog" town was right out of a Louis L'Amour dime novel as was the rustic Moose Lodge, complete with hand hewn, exposed rafters and, of course, a giant, mounted, moose head over a huge stone fireplace. The western attired members, in their scuffed boots and sweat stained hats, were authentic - not fancy fringed-shirted Hollywood wannabees.

Arriving back in Farmington, I found a parking ticket on my windshield. It seemed that everywhere I went, cops were attracted to my Corvette. Not, I'm sure, as enthusiasts, but because they assumed sooner or later the driver was going to race, speed, spin his tires, make noise or all of he above. Their concerns were not without merit. The $3.00 ticket became $100.00 if not paid within 24 hours. Twenty-four or a thousand hours, I wasn't about to pay it. It wasn't the principle of the thing, I just didn't have three bucks to spare!

Early the next morning, I headed for the post office. That was, of course, after I paid my room bill and had a full breakfast. The kindly, middle aged, everybody's-mom-lady-of-the-house, in her gingham dress, wished me good luck. The postmaster told me the mail truck wasn't due for about an hour. I walked to the corner drug store, ordered a coke at the soda fountain and read a three-day old copy of the local paper.

The mail contained nothing for me. Then it was back to the drug store where I used the pay phone to place a collect call to the producer. He refused my call! Well, at least I got gas money to get me this far. California here I come.

As I hit the town's western limit the red light on the police car that had been following me came on. I stopped, got out and walked back to the cruiser.

"You gonna pay that ticket, boy," the rotund, red faced cop spat.

"Not right now, sir. But I will."

"Looks to me like you're leaving town - and that's another crime iffins you gotta outstanding ticket."

"Uh, no sir. I was just going to run a mile or two on the highway. My plugs were beginning to foul from all that town driving I'd been doing and I thought I'd blow 'em out a little. I can't leave until I do the radio interview tonight, I lied."

"Well, go ahead, but if you ain't back in ten minutes, I'm gonna radio to Shiprock to stop you and lock you up. Ya hear?"

It was 25 miles to Shiprock and then another 25 to the Arizona border. Approaching the turn-off to this final town, at my normal cruising speed of 90, I could see two police cars, lights flashing, on the right shoulder. A uniformed officer was standing in the middle of the road, his hand held up, palm forward. I slowed to about 35, shifted to 2nd to wait for the on-coming pickup truck to clear the road block. With the left lane now open, I moved across the yellow line as the officers began waving their hands and shouting. I had to put two wheels on the dirt shoulder to keep from hitting them as they watched, dumbfounded, America's only real sports car rocket away from the them. It was a gamble, but I figured the chances of another cop being between me and the border to be slim.

I'd never experienced 106° - and neither had my Vette! Arizona - hot, dusty and hotter. At those daytime temperatures, I couldn't hold much over 55 and the air blowing on my feet from the cowl vent was so hot I had to close the vent. Gripping the steering wheel caused my hands to sweat, but sticking them out of the window to dry them was to hot to bear. Back on Route 66 at my first gas stop, I learned most cross country drivers only drove at night - when the desert cooled the air. Long before Flagstaff I found a rarity, an air conditioned restaurant, and hunkered down till evening. Because everyone traveled at night, the traffic was the most I'd seen since leaving Houston.

Somewhere in the early morning hours I started down the mountains from Barstow into the San Bernadino valley. The temperature plunged so much I had to stop to paper my radiator so the engine could generate enough heat to warm the interior of the cockpit.

The Los Angeles freeways, aside from the Pennsylvania Turnpike, were the first I'd ever seen. I was so impressed that one morning I awoke around three a.m. just to experience these roads without stop lights. I was especially thrilled to drive over and see "the stack" - a set of over-passes five ramps high! Traffic, during the day light hours, even in 1961, was heavy enough to take the fun out of driving.

****

The foregoing was an actual accounting of the author's experience during the summer of 1961. The author's father, at age 93, and after reading the story, told the following about his trip from Cincinnati to Los Angeles in 1927.

"The first thing we did was purchase a rear view mirror and a water pump because those items didn't come with the Model 'T' Ford." The parts were readily available at a Leo's, Checkers or Western Auto stores for a dollar or two. Soon after installing our travel necessities on our used 1927 Ford roadster, my friend, Phil, and I, both nineteen years of age, headed west. For this adventure, I took vacation time from my job as a draftsman/pattern maker for the Nivison-Weiskopf company in Reading, Ohio.

"We drove to Indianapolis, then through St. Louis, Kansas City, Denver and Salt Lake City. The main road, U.S. 40, was very rough in spots, had minimal gas stations and questionable drinking water. We slung a canvas bag filled with potable water across the hood of the car. The trip was never without adventure with numerous flat tires, other breakdowns and at more than one point, we, along with other travelers, had to ford rivers and streams! Upon entering the Utah desert we stopped to pick up a hitch-hiker - a young man about our age who was trying to get to California where he had been promised a job with the Associated Press. He vowed to send us a press card as soon as he was established - it never arrived.

"Crossing the desert at night I was the first to become drowsy. Phil was driving, the hitch-hiker in the middle and I was next to the passenger door. Because of the remoteness of the roads in these sparsely populated, open plains and mountainous regions of this vast continent, we carried a pearl-handled .25 caliber pistol for protection. There were three of us now, and thinking nothing of it, I turned the handgun over to the stranger to act as guard while I napped and Phil continued driving. Picking up hitch-hikers, much less trusting them with a gun while you slept, would be, today, tantamount to suicide.

"The hitch-hiker was with us for at least one night and two days as we wound our way south to Flagstaff, Arizona where we picked up U.S. Route 66 - in its first year of dedication. In Barstow, California the hitch-hiker left us as he was headed north to San Francisco. Phil and I continued on to Los Angeles."

Author's Note: Early transcontinental routes had miles of unpaved roadway, single lane bridges - or no bridges at all - and few signs or markers. The original Route 66 ran 2400 miles through eight states from Chicago to Santa Monica. This federally designated highway was immortalized by John Steinbeck's, "The Grapes of Wrath," Dorthea Lang's dust bowl photographs, the 60s TV show, "Route 66," and countless travelers such as the author and his father. Today (2003) the original route is all but swallowed up by urban sprawl, obsolescence and Interstates 40, 44 and 55.

About the Author, Chuck Klein

(www.chuckklein.com)

Licensed: Private Investigator,1979

Education: Bachelor of Laws, 1972;

Who's Who in America:, 1998-present

Former Certified: Police Officer and Firefighter

Firearms Editor: P. I. MAGAZINE, 1990 - 2002; Contributing Editor: GUNS & WEAPONS for LAW ENFORCEMENT, 1992 - 1999; Active Member: American Society of Law Enforcement Trainers (ASLET), 1993 - ; Active Member: Int'l Assoc. of Law Enforcement Firearms Instructors (IALEFI), 1999

Local Voices Columnist: THE CINCINNATI ENQUIRER, 2000-2001; Security Columnist: THE AMERICAN ISRAELITE, 2002 Contributing 2nd Amendment Columnist, GUNS & AMMO magazine, 1996

Staff Instructor: TACTICAL DEFENSE INSTITUTE, 2000 (tdiohio.com)

NRA Certified Firearms Instructor: Shotgun, Pistol, Personal Protection and Reloading, 1970 -

Other information

Woodward High School Class of 1960

Ohio v. Feely: Ohio C.C.W. court case with Constitutional issues (Klein, et. al. v. Leis, et. al.)

Books by Chuck Klein:

THE WAY IT WAS,
Nostalgic Tales of Hot Rods and Romance

A collection of historically and technically correct, ILLUSTRATED short stories set in 1950s America many of which are unpublished

THE POWER OF GOD

A powerful novel exposing a de facto hole in America's civil defense

CREATIVITY HANDBOOK

A Formula for Originating Ideas

KLEIN'S C.C.W. HANDBOOK

The Requisite for those who Carry Concealed Weapons

KLEIN'S UNIFORM FIREARMS MANUAL

A Manual for Private Sector Detectives and Security Agents

CIRCA 1957

A coming-of-age novel set during the birth of rock & roll and hot rodding

INSTINCT COMBAT SHOOTING

Defensive Handgunning for Police and Personal Protection

FIREARMS INSTRUCTOR COURSE

Correspondence course to become a Certified Firearms Instructor

LINES OF DEFENSE
Police Ideology and the Constitution

This hard hitting, tell-it-like-it-is police academy text book will surely raise hackles and stir controversy

Route 66 books by Michael Lund

Growing Up on Route 66 – Michael Lund (2000) ISBN 1-888725-31-1 Novel evoking fond memories of what it was like to grow up alongside "America's Highway" in 20th Century Missouri. (paperback) 5x8 260 pp, $14.95

Route 66 Kids – Michael Lund (2002) ISBN 1-888725-70-2 Sequel to *Growing Up on Route 66*, continuing memories of what it was like to grow up alongside "America's Highway" in 20th Century Missouri. (paperback) 5x8 270 pp, $14.95

A Left-hander on Route 66--Michael Lund (2003) ISBN 1-888725-88-5. Twenty years after the fact, left-hander Hugh Noone appeals a wrongful conviction that detoured him from "America's Main Street" and put him in jail. But revealing the details of the past and effecting a resolution of his case mean a dramatic rearrangement of his world, including troubled relationships with three women: Linda Roy, Patty Simpson, and Karen Murphy. 5x8 270 pp, $14.95

Route 66 Spring-- Michael Lund (2004) ISBN: 1-888725-98-2. The lives of four young Missourians are changed when a bottle comes to the surface of one of the state's many natural springs. Inside is a letter written by a girl a dozen years after the end of the Civil War. Lucy Rivers Johns ' epistle contains a sad story of family failure and a powerful plea for help. This message from the last century crystallizes the individual frustrations of Janet Masters, Freddy Sills, Louis Clark, and Roberta Green, another group of Route 66 kids. Their response to the past charts a bold path into the future, a path inspired by the Mother Road itself. 5x8 270 pp, 14.95.

Miss Route 66--Michael Lund (2004) ISBN 1-888725-96-6. In the fourth novel of Michael Lund's Route 66 Novel Series, Susan Bell tells the story of her candidacy in Fairfield, Missouri's annual beauty contest. Now married and with teenage children in St. Louis, she recounts her youthful adventure in this small town along "America's Highway."   At the same time, she plans a return to Fairfield in order to right injustices she feels were done to some young contestants in the Miss Route 66 Pageant.   5x8, 260 pp, $14.95 **Audiobook** on 5 CD's ISBN 1-888725-12-5 $24.95

Route 66 to Vietnam Michael Lund (2004) ISBN 1-59630-000-0 This novel takes characters from earlier works in the Route 66 Novel Series farther west than Los Angeles, official destination of the famous highway, Route 66. Mark Landon and Billy Rhodes find the values they grew up on challenged by America's role in Southeast Asia. But elements of their upbringing represented by the Mother Road also sustain them in ways they could never have anticipated. . (paperback) 5x8, 270 pp, $14.95.

AudioBook on CD — Route 66 to Vietnam ISBN: 1-59630-011-6 Michael Lund's fictional commentary from the viewpoint of a draftee. by Michael Lund unabridged 6 CD's --9 hours running time. $24.95

Route 66 Chapel Michael Lund (2006) ISBN 1-59630-012-4 Route 66 Chapel, Michael Lund (2006) (paperback) 5x8 260 pp, $14.95. When the forces of progress threaten the foundation of smalltown life — a small church — five senior citizens, a mysterious newcomer, and one young couple band together in an unlikely campaign to save it. The embattled meeting point of old and new is Route 66 Chapel, a building curiously linked to America's "Mother Road."

Route 66 Choir-- A Comedy (2010)Michael Lund ISBN 9781596300583 284 pp 5" x 8" 14.95 In Route 66 Choir Stanley Measure takes early retirement just before September 11, 2001, and his impulsive decisions participate in an unraveling of confidence in the American way of life. His wife Felicia finds that everything she holds dear is in danger of coming apart: her marriage, her church, her business, and even her country. Who or what can orchestrate the recovery of harmony necessary to sustain the spirit of the Mother Road?

Route 66 Bride (Fall 2010)

BeachHouse Books
PO Box 7151
Chesterfield, MO 63006-7151
(636) 394-4950
www.beachhousebooks.com

www.beachhousebooks.com

www.ingramcontent.com/pod-product-compliance
Lightning Source LLC
Chambersburg PA
CBHW071205260626
47162CB00003B/1175